AURORA BLAZE

A Long Journey Nowhere

Copyright © 2023 by Aurora Blaze

All rights reserved. No part of this publication may be reproduced, stored or transmitted in any form or by any means, electronic, mechanical, photocopying, recording, scanning, or otherwise without written permission from the publisher. It is illegal to copy this book, post it to a website, or distribute it by any other means without permission.

This novel is entirely a work of fiction. The names, characters and incidents portrayed in it are the work of the author's imagination. Any resemblance to actual persons, living or dead, events or localities is entirely coincidental.

Aurora Blaze asserts the moral right to be identified as the author of this work.

First edition

This book was professionally typeset on Reedsy. Find out more at reedsy.com

Contents

Authors Note — iv
Chapter 1 "The Last Bus Home" — 1
Chapter 2 "The Notebook" — 11
Chapter 3 "The Thief" — 18
Chapter 4 "The Mercenaries Tail!" — 28
Chapter 5 "A Long Way From Home" — 39
Chapter 6 "The Abandoned City" — 47
Chapter 7 "Cosmic Despair" — 60
Chapter 8 "The Great Escape!" — 71
Chapter 9 "The Battle In The Sky!" — 80
Chapter 10 "The Consequences of Love" — 88
Chapter 11 "Make Love Not War" — 101
Chapter 12 "From Armen With Love" — 110
Chapter 13 "Homeward-Bound" — 116
Chapter 14 "Home Sweet Home" — 124
Chapter 15 "A Long Journey Nowhere" — 134
Thank you! — 145

Authors Note

Dear Reader,

    I'm excited to introduce my debut book, a labor of love exploring themes of love, perseverance, and hope amidst life's darkest trials. The characters' journeys demonstrate the incredible power of love to overcome even the toughest challenges. I invite you to interpret and derive your own meanings from the story. Thank you for supporting my work, and I can't wait to connect with you at the end of the book.

    Best regards,
    Aurora Blaze

Chapter 1 "The Last Bus Home"

I trudge down the desolate sidewalk with my hands in my black bomber jacket, my long black hair blowing in the wind, haunted by my regrets. Night after night, I am forced to brave the darkness and navigate my way through the treacherous streets of this crime-infested city after days of unfulfilling, stressful work. The moon casts an eerie glow over the tops of the buildings, painting the sky with a surreal palette of silvery hues. It's a sight to behold, reminiscent of a classic noir film, except I'm far from the charismatic, suave detective archetype.

Each night, the bus stop seems to drift further and further away, and the journey becomes increasingly perilous. The lurking danger is palpable, and the slightest rustle in the shadows sends shivers down my spine and causes my light brown skin to break into a cold sweat. Recent news of a series of murders has only added to the tension. The latest victim was found partially devoured, with strange bite marks covering his mutilated body. It's believed that there's a humanoid killer on the loose, preying on unsuspecting victims and robbing and consuming them.

Walking towards the bus stop, my heart racing, I can't help but feel like a sitting duck. The killer's pattern of targeting 20-something loners who take public transit late at night, regardless of gender, hits a little too close to home. It's a disturbing thought, but a part of me finds it strangely funny. Eh, I doubt I would ever actually encounter such a situation, as I do my best to avoid any interactions with people in general due to my anxiety disorder's favorite pastime of edging a panic attack when I'm around people too long. Since the pointless war fought a few years back over some stupid natural resource, an increasing number of them have migrated to New Colombia, and I am still struggling to adjust to their presence.

The relentless sense of loneliness would get to me before any humanoid does. Lately, things have been pretty rough, to the point where it's a miracle that I'm even able to walk around right now. However, despite this, I can't lose sight of my main objective: make it home alive. Fortunately, my sense of humor provides some relief, preventing me from completely succumbing to despair. I can't imagine how I would cope without it.

As I approach the bench at the bus stop, I notice that the streetlights are flickering. I begin to feel like I'm being watched, and a shiver of fear travels up my spine. Suddenly, the streetlights go out, plunging me into a sea of darkness. The sole streetlight above me now acts as a spotlight, illuminating me like a target for an untimely demise. Paranoia sets in, and I begin to sweat profusely from every pore.

Desperately seeking a sign of hope, I scan the black void, but to no avail. The sensation of being watched grows stronger, and I feel like something is breathing down my neck. Summoning the courage of my last day in kindergarten, where I fought like a warrior and sent many bullies running, I turn to face the darkness. There's nothing there, but I still feel a presence.

Suddenly, after what feels like an eternity, I catch sight of the distant headlights and the screeching sound of a bus. Relief floods through me, but I remain wary, knowing that my pursuer could easily drag me into a dark alleyway unnoticed. As the blue metallic bus approaches like a divine savior, I hastily retrieve my pass and flag it down. Boarding the bus, I present my pass to the driver before proceeding to the back.

The bus was relatively empty, with only a handful of passengers aboard; two humans and three humanoids. Hastening past the rows occupied by the humanoids, I made my way to the rear of the bus. Collapsing against the cold window, closing my eyes in the hopes of stealing some much-needed rest. A grueling seven-hour ride lay ahead of me until I reached the bus stop closest to my home, and I couldn't afford to be fatigued for work the next day.

While I drifted off to sleep on the bus, I was unaware of the Bunny girl humanoid who had taken the seat across from me. I woke up two hours later to find her staring at me from the corner of her eye, holding a notebook in her lap. Her appearance was striking: long white hair, floppy ears atop her head with black piercings, a black plastic headband, and a solid black choker. Her pinkish-red eyes and very pale skin tone added to her unique look. She wore a solid black midi sundress, adorned with matching black bulky bracelets, and stood at an impressive 6'0".

Despite my shyness, I couldn't resist stealing glances at her because she was beautiful. Her gaze was intense, making me feel a bit uneasy and causing me to retreat toward the window. Although I wanted to speak to her, my nerves held me back. After a moment of silence, she finally broke the ice.

"Excuse me if this is too forward, but would you mind coming over here?" she asked in a friendly and cheerful tone.

"Me? I nervously replied. She nodded, and my feet moved on their own.

"Would you like to sit next to me? She gestures, patting the seat next to her "You look like a ball of anxiety, so I was wondering if you'd like some company,". I was a bit hesitant but accepted her offer, plopping down right next to her.

After a few moments of uncomfortable silence, she broke it with a sudden question. "So, uh what's your name?" she asked, looking at me curiously.

I felt my heart skip a beat as I turned to look at her. The sight of her bunny ears and fluffy tail made me feel both fascinated and intimidated. "My name is Jon," I managed to mutter out nervously.

"Is it the J-O-H-N way or the degenerate without the H way?"

"I chuckled and relaxed my shoulders I respond "The degenerate way", feeling more at ease." "So, what's your name?"

"My name is Lilith," she said, and I couldn't help but feel a spark of curiosity toward this strange and intriguing Bunny girl sitting next to me.

Chapter 1 "The Last Bus Home"

"What a pretty name,"

She perked up a bit with a smile. "Thank you, I like your name too. It's straight and to the point."

With the ice broken, Lilith and I delved into our interests, quickly discovering that we shared a love for music, movies, and video games. We excitedly discussed our favorite horror films. Lilith had a particular passion for horror slasher films but bemoaned the lack of strong female villains in the genre.

"I know what you mean," I nodded in agreement. "But have you seen some of the foreign horror films? They have some great female slasher villains."

As I shared a few of my favorite foreign horror films featuring female protagonists and antagonists, Lilith's eyes lit up with interest. We continued chatting until we reached Lilith's stop, and before I knew it, she gave me her phone number and urged me to text her. She told me that she needed to hurry and grab something to eat before her favorite restaurant closed, and then she ran off.

When she rushed off the bus, I couldn't help but notice her cute, fluffy cotton tail swaying with each step. Despite my best efforts to keep my gaze locked on her tail, I found myself looking down at her legs and immediately felt ashamed and flustered.

Once I got home and climbed into bed, my mind kept drifting back to her. I couldn't stop thinking about her for the rest of the night. As I lay there staring at the ceiling, a mix of excitement and anxiety built up inside me. I was determined to text her and see where things would go from there but you know anxiety wouldn't let me.

* * *

The next day, I finally managed to muster the courage to text her, and to my delight, she responded promptly. We ended up texting back and forth the entire day, fueling my excitement to see her again. And soon enough, we went on our first date to a posh restaurant run by humanoids. Everything just fell into place - we were having a great time, the food was exquisite, and our conversation flowed effortlessly. It was then that we shared our first kiss, and I felt my heart skip a beat as she wrapped her arms around me, holding me close. I felt like I was melting in her embrace, unable to contain my overwhelming emotions.

Reluctantly, she let me go and said her goodbyes. As she walked away, I waved goodbye, still in awe of what had just happened. But as soon as she was out of sight, I collapsed in a cartoonish fashion, unable to believe what had just transpired. A humanoid wolf waiter rushed over to check on me and help me up. I assured him I was fine, left a generous tip, and made my way out of the restaurant Awkwardly.

After that unforgettable first date, I was on cloud nine. Lilith was incredible, and I couldn't believe my good fortune in meeting her.

Being with her brought me an overwhelming sense of calm that made my anxieties and depression fade away. Even though my anxiety disorder persisted, she helped me manage it better.

Her presence and unwavering support were transformative, changing the way I perceived humanoids. Before meeting her, I was consumed by fear and prejudice, unable to see past their differences and see them as individuals. Only scary monsters that kind of resemble humans. But Lilith, with her open heart and compassionate spirit, showed me a different way.

She introduced me to a diverse array of humanoids from various backgrounds and cultures, taking the time to educate me about their customs and beliefs. I learned about their struggles and triumphs, their joys and sorrows. Through her guidance, It was only then I began to see their humanity and recognize the beauty in our differences.

Lilith's patience and willingness to answer my endless questions helped me overcome the barriers I had built around myself. I started to feel more at ease with humanoids than with regular humans, something I never thought was possible. Her influence had a ripple effect, and I found myself more open-minded and accepting of others, regardless of their species or background.

Thanks to Lilith's insistence, a world of incredible experiences and opportunities has opened up for me. As a result, I landed a new job as a lead artist for a self-published romance graphic novel by a 23-year-old trans girl named Sal, who happens to be a raccoon humanoid who I wound up becoming good friends with. Lilith recommended the novel to me, and after checking out the artwork and discovering they were looking for a replacement lead artist, I applied for the position. I am finally able to put my incomplete art degree to good use, and I couldn't be happier with my new job. Not only does it pay more, but it's also less stressful and it allowed me to get my first car. Lilith coined it the rust mobile(It wasn't that bad).

As Lilith and I continued to text and talk on the phone every day, our relationship deepened, and we found ourselves planning date after date. Whether it was our 20th or 100th date, I lost track. All I knew was that I cherished every moment spent with her.

* * *

One day, we decided to go on a picnic in the park, and I spent the entire morning preparing for it. I wanted to impress Lilith and show her how much she meant to me. When I arrived at the park, Lilith was already there with a blanket and a basket of food. She looked stunning in a floral dress, and I couldn't help feeling nervous in her presence.

We sat down on the blanket and started eating the delicious food she had packed. As we ate, we talked about everything and anything, and the conversations were incredible. My favorite one was when I complained about how modern Triple-A games rely too much on bloat and fancy graphics and are not fun.

She responded by telling me to stop buying them and play Indies instead. I retorted by saying that indies don't do it for me, at least not the ones I've played and that I'd rather play retro games even though they're expensive.

"You need to let go of the past- enjoy new things," Lilith responded. "While they are good, a lot of them are dated, and paying hundreds of dollars for them is insane. Just like I said, indie games have you covered because there is a lot that has what makes those games good and has modern polish."

"Okay, I'll give it a try, but you've got to help me," I said.

"I've got you," A smile goes across her face.

After we finished eating, we lay down on the blanket and looked up at the clouds. Lilith pointed out the different shapes, and we giggled about how silly they looked. It was a perfect day, and I felt grateful to have such a wonderful person in my life.

Before I knew it, the sun was starting to set, and I knew it was time to make my move. I turned to Lilith and told her how much I enjoyed spending time with her and how much she meant to me. She smiled and leaned in for a kiss. Our lips met, and it felt like fireworks were going off all around us. It was magical, and I knew at that moment on that I was deeply in love with her.

We continued to date for several months, and each date was better than the last. We went to museums, concerts, and even took a trip to the beach (I hate sand). It was like we were living in a fairy tale, and I never wanted it to end. She helped me really come into myself.
   I no longer had as much anxiety, stress, and depression as I use to. No longer did I take each day I live for granite, living each to the fullest no matter what.

Eventually, I knew I had to tell Lilith how I felt. I had fallen head over heels in love with her, and I couldn't imagine my life without her. We went to her favorite restaurant, and as we ate, I poured my heart out to her. I told her that I loved her and wanted to spend the rest of my life with her.

As Lilith looked at me with tears in her eyes, she whispered the words, "I love you too." It was a moment of pure bliss, and I knew that I had found my soulmate. From that day on, it felt like we were inseparable, and our love continued to blossom with each passing moment. We made the decision to move in together but agreed to wait another year before tying the knot, as much as we both wanted to get married right away.

* * *

One evening, after a long day at work, I came home to find Lilith already there, looking a little worse for wear. She had bruises on her arms and a small cut on her forehead. Concerned, I asked her what had happened and offered to tend to her wounds. At first, she seemed hesitant to say anything, but eventually, she explained that she had taken a bad fall at work and assured me that it was nothing to worry about.

Despite her reassurances, I couldn't shake the feeling that something was off. I noticed that she seemed a bit nervous and avoided making eye contact. I asked her if there was anything else she wanted to tell me, but she shook her head and insisted that everything was fine. At that moment, I decided to trust her and let the matter go, but I couldn't help but wonder if there was more to the story.

Chapter 2 "The Notebook"

Lilith's behavior began to change as the months passed. She would come home late with a foul smell on her clothes and wear the big black bulky bracelets she had on when we first met all the time. At first, I didn't think much of it and still loved her just the same. But as time went on, she became more distant and cold. She barely communicated with me, and when she did, it was only to stare blankly at the ceiling.

Over time the smell on her clothes became worse, and even the washing machine began to smell bad. I knew something was wrong, so I confronted her about it. She quickly explained that the club had lost their cook, so she had to help prepare meat in the kitchen, even though she was just a waitress. I didn't entirely believe her, but I tried to convince myself that I was just overthinking things.

She promised to come home earlier and spend more time with me, and she did keep her word. But despite her efforts, things didn't feel the same. I couldn't shake off the feeling that something was off. I started to feel uncomfortable around her, but I tried to brush it off as my anxiety disorder acting up again.

One night, we watched a thriller movie together about a serial killer. We had a playful argument about the unrealistic aspects of the movie, but Lilith's extensive knowledge of serial killers and her disturbing way of talking about them made me extremely uncomfortable. As we continued to watch the movie, Lilith leaned over to me and said, "You know, not all serial killers are bad people. Some of them are just delusional and have a good reason for what they do. They have demons they have to fight, just like everyone else."

I stared at her in shock, my anxiety rising with every word she spoke. "What are you talking about? Serial killers are murderers, they kill innocent people for no reason!" I exclaimed.

Lilith's eyes grew sad as she tried to explain her point of view. "I'm not saying what they do is right, but sometimes things happen to them that make them snap. They feel like they have to do what they do to survive, or to protect themselves or others."

I couldn't believe what I was hearing. Was Lilith actually sympathizing with serial killers? My mind raced as I tried to make sense of what she was saying. "I don't know how you can say that," I said, my voice shaking with anger and fear. "Innocent people have lost their lives because of these monsters. How can you defend them?"

Lilith looked away, her eyes filling with tears. "I'm not defending them, I'm just saying that there might be more to their stories than we know. It's not black and white, there are always shades of gray."

Chapter 2 "The Notebook"

But I couldn't listen to her anymore. My anxiety was spiraling out of control, and I couldn't be around someone who could justify the actions of serial killers. I got up from the couch and walked out of the room, leaving Lilith alone with her thoughts. Despite trying to convince myself that she was simply interested in true crime, I couldn't shake the nagging feeling that something was off and that Lilith might have been involved with something sinister.

* * *

Lilith's behavior had become increasingly aloof and strange as a few more months passed. I just couldn't shake the feeling that she was keeping something from me. She started to respond often with one-word answers or stare at me blankly as if lost in thought. Despite my best efforts to connect with her, she remained elusive.

One day, I won a radio sweepstakes and decided to take Lilith out on a rare date. We went to a fancy restaurant, and for a brief moment, it seemed like things were getting better. She was laughing and smiling, and we had a great time. However, the feeling didn't last long. After the date, Lilith started coming home later and later until she stopped coming home altogether.

Days went by without any word from her, and I began to worry. Finally, I decided to investigate by letting myself into her apartment while she was at work. As I searched through her belongings, I found nothing out of the ordinary until I accidentally knocked over a dresser and found a notebook hidden behind it. It was the same notebook she had on the bus when we first met. Curious, I picked it up.

When I opened the notebook, I was horrified to see a record of the victims of the humanoid serial killer that was still on the loose. The list included their names, the exact locations where they had met their end, and the date and time down to the hour. I tried to convince myself that it couldn't be true, but as I read further, my heart sank. There, scratched out with a pen, was my name, dated two and a half years ago.

The notebook entries stopped at my name before continuing again, starting back seven months ago. As I pored over the meticulous details, including the victims' age, height, weight, and whether they had any family or friends (most, if not all, didn't), I heard the sound of the front door opening, and Lilith walked in covered in blood from a recent victim, crying. As Lilith walked into the apartment covered in blood, I could see the pain and sadness etched on her face. She was crying, but the tears didn't make her look vulnerable; they only made her seem more dangerous. I could tell that she was struggling to keep herself together, and it broke my heart to see her like this.

But what broke my heart, even more, was the realization that she was a killer. The woman I had fallen in love with, the one I had thought was just a little strange, was a murderer. It was like a nightmare coming to life, and I couldn't wrap my head around it. I felt like I didn't even know her, and the thought of what she had done made me sick to my stomach. I quickly hid and managed to slip past Lilith with the notebook. Not knowing what to do, I was lost, confused, and heartbroken. I was hysterical and ran home, pathetically falling over myself and breaking my cell phone before getting up again, a bit bloodied. As soon as I got home, I hunkered down in a closet and cried.

Over the next few days, I avoided Lilith's attempts to reach me, feeling like I was hiding from a predator. I was afraid to confront her because I knew she was much stronger than me. I was sad, alone, and a prisoner

Chapter 2 "The Notebook"

of my own mind. I was too afraid to do anything, and I refused what was right in front of me to believe she was capable of such awful things. I couldn't process it, so I didn't seek any help, which is what any reasonable person would have done. Instead, I just hid in my house, feeling despair, and sometimes, I didn't move or eat for days. A few times, she almost managed to break into my house through a window in my basement, ripping it out and climbing in, yelling for me, and crying before leaving.

* * *

Finally, I reached my breaking point. During a power outage, she broke in, and I found myself hiding under the floorboards while she rummaged through the house looking for me. I heard slow, careful footsteps above me and felt the blood from Lilith's recent victim dripping between the floorboards onto my face. It smelled fresh, as the metallic smell filled my nose. I knew I had to take action. So, the next day when the coast was clear, I climbed out of my kitchen floorboards and tried to call the police, but all the lines were still down due to the power outage. I remembered that my cell phone had been snapped in half. After pondering for a moment on what to do, I decided to drive to the police station, feeling extremely foolish for not taking action sooner. I summon the little courage I had and left the house with the notebook

* * *

I sat trembling in the car, my fingers wrapped tightly around the notebook filled with Lilith's victims' names. Tears streamed down my face, and my heart shattered into a million pieces. The courage to stop Lilith eluded me; her grip on me was too strong.

Suddenly, the cold barrel of a gun pressed against the back of my head, and fear jolted through me like a bolt of lightning. Lilith had caught me, and now she had me at gunpoint. With shaking hands, I handed over the notebook.

Through my tears, Lilith began to speak. Her words were unexpected, confessing that she had fallen deeply in love with me on our first night together, despite my name being in the notebook. But the tenderness in her words quickly faded, and she became callous once more as if knowing what she must do. Despite my desperate pleas for mercy, she instructed me to get into the backseat of the car, and I knew then that she intended to take me to a deserted part of town and murder me like her previous victims.

I mustered my courage and asked, "Why are you doing this?" Lilith's response was evasive, and she avoided giving me a direct answer. Instead, she took me down memory lane, reminiscing about the happy times we shared, like the night we first met and the deep connection we had. Though I cherished those good moments, the confusion and fear of what she had done or was going to do to me lingered.

* * *

Lilith's driving became increasingly erratic, and I realized she was becoming unstable and unpredictable. Despite our past connection, I tried to reason with her, pleading for my life and asking her to reconsider. But her mind was made up, and I was left feeling hopeless and desperate for a way out.

As we approached a cliff side with no guardrails, I saw an opportunity to escape, though it was a long shot. Without hesitation, I unlocked the door and jumped out of the moving car. Lilith fired her gun twice, but fortunately, she missed, and I tumbled down the cliff into the water below.

As I plunged into the water, Lilith's screams echoed above, promising to hunt me down to the ends of the earth. Fear and adrenaline still pulsed through my veins, but I forced myself to push through the overwhelming sensations and focus on staying alive. Every stroke was frantic as I searched for any sign of dry land, but the unyielding current relentlessly dragged me further into the depths of the open ocean. Exhaustion slowly crept over me, and my limbs felt as fragile as glass, and my breathing became shallow and labored. But I refused to give up and kept fighting with every ounce of energy I had left. As a massive wave loomed over me, I knew it was too late to escape, and it engulfed me, pulling me into unconsciousness.

Chapter 3 "The Thief"

When I finally regained consciousness, my head was pounding, and I found myself in unfamiliar surroundings - trapped in the quarters of a ship, alongside a beautiful yet enigmatic fox girl. My throat felt raw, and my mind was racing with a million questions, but I struggled to find the words to voice them.

"Who are you?" I managed to croak out.

I looked into the fox girl's striking brown eyes and took in her light brown skin, I felt the gravity of the situation sink in. "I'm Amara, and you're in deep trouble," she said, her words heavy with concern. Fear washed over me as I contemplated our fate.

Amara's somber expression matched the weight of her words as she explained that we were aboard a slave ship, bound for a distant land where we would be sold to the highest bidder. The very idea of being treated as someone's property filled me with rage, but I knew that we were utterly powerless to resist. As despair set in, I found myself

Chapter 3 "The Thief"

grappling with the harsh reality of our dire predicament. I didn't even have time to process Lilith, and now I find myself in this situation. At this moment, I am overcome with a strong sense of dread.

But with a hopeful glimmer in her eyes, Amara confided in me that she was an experienced thief who had spent weeks carefully planning her escape. As she spoke, she lifted her plastic yellow headband to reveal a small, inconspicuous tracker hidden underneath. The yellow band sat atop her head in front of two big pointy black fox ears with white tips, each one adorned with two golden rings.

Amara explained that this tracker was one of her keys to freedom, as it was designed to send a distress signal to her old mercenary friends. However, it had been a couple of weeks since she activated it, and she wasn't sure if it was still working.

She had a distinctive appearance with long curly black hair, a yellow plastic headband, a yellow rhinestone necklace, and a big fluffy black and white fox tail. She wore a red leather jacket, a red skirt, black thigh-high socks, a black undershirt, and brown loafers. Despite her situation, she seemed to take pride in her appearance and stood out because of it.

As I observed her, I couldn't help but feel hopeful as well. Amara's confidence and resourcefulness gave me faith that we could escape our captivity.

Even though the possibility of the mercs showing up was uncertain, Amara was not willing to give up hope. She was determined to escape and encouraged me to help her look for alternative ways out of the ship. As we worked together, Amara opened up to me about her past.

Amara's birth was the product of a rare union between a humanoid fox and a human, resulting in a unique lineage that sets her apart from others of her kind. Her darker complexion, a trait inherited from her human side, distinguishes her from other humanoid foxes and made her a target of discrimination and exclusion. As a result of being ostracized from humanoid fox society, Amara had to resort to thievery as a means of survival and wound up being one of the most successful in the world.

Amara told me her luck finally ran out when she made the grave mistake of attempting to steal from the wrong individuals She was captured and Since she would fetch a high price for her skills they sold her to human trafficking pirates. Despite the inhumane treatment she received, Amara's spirit remained unbroken, and she was determined to fight for her freedom. Witnessing her incredible strength and resilience, I couldn't help but feel inspired to support her in any way I could.

* * *

When we plotted our escape, Amara's optimism was infectious, but soon we realized that breaking free from the slave ship was not going to be easy. The ship was heavily guarded, and the crew was merciless, leaving us no choice but to spend our days in captivity and get to know each other on a much deeper level.

As we sat and talked, I opened up to Amara about the events that led me to be on the ship. I shared with her the terrifying experience of discovering that my girlfriend was a serial killer who tried to murder me. Amara listened intently, her eyes filled with shock and disbelief.

"I can't even imagine what that must have been like for you," Amara said reassuringly. "But you're not alone."

Her words gave me hope, and I felt a connection with her that I hadn't expected. Despite the perilous situation, we found ourselves in, we discovered solace in our mutual passion for science and space exploration. As we worked on devising an escape plan, Amara and I engaged in deep conversations that covered a wide range of topics.

We delved into the mysteries of marine biology and pondered the secrets hidden in the depths of the ocean. Our discussions also centered on the vastness of the universe, which filled us with wonder and amazement.

Amara's aptitude for math proved invaluable during our planning sessions, while I struggled in that area. Nevertheless, we collaborated, utilizing each other's strengths to create a successful escape strategy.

Amidst the urgency of our situation, we continued to find solace in the common bond of our thirst for knowledge - something that Lilith and I didn't share, even though she was the smarter one between the two of us.

It was a welcomed distraction from our primary objective of escaping, but we remained steadfast in our quest to find a way out. Time was not on our side, and we knew that we had to act quickly to secure our freedom. But it fostered a sense of camaraderie and hope, which we clung to tightly.

However, that hope dwindled as time went on, and the harsh conditions of our confinement began to take a toll on our fellow captives. One by one, they succumbed to disease and despair, leaving only Amara and me to endure the brutal journey. Nevertheless, we remained resolute in our determination to break free.

But hope was in short supply, and it seemed that our situation was becoming increasingly dire. That was until one night when we were lying in our cramped quarters, with nothing but the creaking of the ship and the sound of our breathing to break the silence. Suddenly, Amara sat up, her eyes bright with a newfound determination.

"I've got an idea," exclaimed Amara, causing me to fall out of bed. Her brown eyes glinted with newfound hope as she spoke loudly. While I was writhing on the floor with a foreign object lodged inside me where it shouldn't be.

She went on to explain her plan in detail, her voice low and urgent. We would need to move quickly and quietly, avoiding the guards and the crew as much as possible. But if we could pull it off, we would have a chance to escape.

The following day, we put our plan into action. Amara utilized her remarkable thievery abilities to escape the quarters and evade the guards undetected. She proceeded to infiltrate the captain's quarters and successfully acquired the map, all while taking great care to avoid detection. Despite the inherent danger, Amara managed to slip out unnoticed.

With the map in our hands, we could see the layout of the ship and plan our escape route. We knew where the guards were stationed and which areas would be the most difficult to navigate. It was still a daunting task, but we were more prepared than ever before.

As the days went by, we continued to work on our plan, refining it and making sure that we were ready for anything. Finally, the night arrived, and we put everything into action. We moved quickly and quietly, slipping past guards and hiding in the shadows.

But as we made our way to the deck, we were suddenly confronted by a group of armed guards. They had somehow discovered our plan, and our escape had been foiled. Our hearts sank as we realized that we were back to square one, trapped once again on the slave ship.

We were thrown back into our quarters, and our spirits were crushed. But we refused to give up. We knew that we had to keep trying if we wanted to escape and regain our freedom. As we lay in our cramped quarters once again, Amara and I vowed to never give up until we were free. In the days that followed, Amara and I tried every possible escape plan we could think of. We spent hours studying the ship's layout, trying to find weaknesses and vulnerabilities that we could exploit.

Our first attempt was to create a distraction by starting a fire in one of the storage rooms. We managed to sneak in and light a small flame, but it quickly grew out of control, and we were forced to flee before we could cause too much damage.

Our second attempt was to overpower one of the guards and steal his keys. We managed to sneak up on a guard during one of his rounds, but he was stronger than we anticipated, and we were no match for him.

Our third escape attempt was undoubtedly the most audacious. Frustrated with our previous failed attempts, we hatched a plan to create a diversion by causing chaos on the deck. After managing to sneak out of our quarters undetected, we found ourselves on the open-air deck armed with a fake gun we made. Amara held the guard hostage, while we made a ruckus, shouting and causing a commotion.

The plan worked, and we managed to attract the attention of the guards successfully. Within moments, they descended upon us, and amid the ensuing chaos, we made a daring attempt to escape. Unfortunately, luck was not on our side as the guards soon discovered that the gun we had used to intimidate them was fake when it fell apart. Our hopes of freedom were crushed once again. However, despite the repeated setbacks, we refused to give up. Our determination to escape only grew stronger as we knew we had to keep trying until we found a way out.

The days turned into weeks, we continued to rack our brains for new escape plans, trying every possible angle we could think of. However, no matter how meticulously we plotted or how carefully we executed our schemes, each attempt was foiled before we could make any significant progress.

After a while, the pirates were furious with us for our repeated attempts to escape. Our constant scheming and foiled plans had pushed their patience to the limit. We could see the anger in their eyes every time they caught us, and the punishment they meted out became increasingly severe.

We knew that we had become a thorn in their side. But despite the risks, we refused to give up our fight for freedom. We knew that we had to keep trying, even if it meant incurring the wrath of our captors. We refused to be deterred, We continued to plot and plan, knowing that we had to seize every opportunity that presented itself if we were to ever escape the clutches of our captors.

**

Chapter 3 "The Thief"

One sunny day, as we were taking our daily allowed walk around the ship's deck, we spotted a small boat at the far end. It was old and rusty, but it was our only chance at escaping the prison that had been our home for too long. We knew the risks, but we couldn't let this opportunity slip away.

That night, we snuck out of our quarters and made our way to the boat, hearts pounding with anticipation. With trembling hands, we untied the rope and pushed the boat away from the ship. The silence was deafening as we rowed away, the moon guiding us toward our freedom.

Hours passed, and the exhaustion and fear began to take their toll on us. But we were determined to keep rowing, to keep moving forward. The sun began to rise, and we knew we were getting closer to our goal. We hugged each other, tears of relief and happiness streaming down our faces.

But then, we heard it. The sound of an engine coming from behind us. We turned around, and our hearts sank as we saw a speedboat full of armed guards chasing after us. They fired a warning shot, and we knew we were in trouble.

In a desperate attempt to escape, we jumped into the water and started swimming. The cold water embraced us, and we could hear our hearts pounding in our ears. I swam towards Amara, but before I could reach her, I heard a gunshot. Amara cried out in pain, and I turned around to see her sinking into the water. I grabbed her arm and pulled her towards me, but it was too late. The guards were upon us, and they were not merciful.

They pulled us back towards the ship, their hands grabbing at us and pulling us out of the water. We struggled against them, but it was useless. They were too many, too strong. And as they dragged us back to our quarters, I knew that our dream of freedom had been shattered forever. The rough stone walls seemed to close in on me, suffocating me with their oppressive presence. I struggled to keep up with the guards' pace, my legs heavy and leaden with fatigue.

Beside me, Amara's breathing was shallow and ragged, and my heart clenched with worry. I couldn't bear to lose her, not after everything we had been through. As we stumbled along, I pulled her close to me, holding her tight in my arms. Her skin was cool and clammy against mine, and I could feel her heart beating erratically beneath her chest. I whispered words of comfort to her, telling her how much I loved her and that everything would be okay, even though I wasn't sure if it would be.

The journey back to the quarters seemed to take forever, each step more agonizing than the last. The guards were silent, their faces blank and unreadable, but I could sense their disapproval and disdain for us. I knew we were in for a rough time once we arrived, but I didn't care. All I cared about was Amara, and making sure she was safe and protected from whatever horrors awaited us.

Chapter 3 "The Thief"

Chapter 4 "The Mercenaries Tail!"

The air was thick with the smell of sweat and despair as I sat huddled in the corner of our oppressive quarters. The walls were closing in on me, suffocating me with their weight. I longed to escape, but the crew had increased their guard, making it almost impossible to leave. The reinforced door and heightened monitoring had made it even more difficult, adding to my sense of hopelessness.

But even in the depths of despair, a glimmer of hope shone through. I refused to give up on Amara or our shared dream of freedom. We had come too far to surrender now, and I was determined to keep fighting until we escaped the grasp of our captors.

I tended to Amara's wounds as best I could, gently cleaning and dressing them. I prayed for her recovery, hoping that she would wake up soon. Despite feeling alone and overwhelmed, I found comfort in talking to her and sharing my past, fears, and regrets, even though she remained unconscious. I confided to her about my past and my once-profound affection for Lilith, the woman who had once held my heart.

As I recounted the months and years that had led us to this point, a jumbled mix of sadness and anger overwhelmed me. Memories of our passionate and intense relationship, filled with adventure and excitement, came flooding back. But the recollection was bittersweet, as it reminded me of the moment when Lilith had attempted to take my life.

Although a part of me still longed for Lilith and the life we had once shared, I realized that returning to that past was impossible. I shifted my focus to the present and made it my mission to assist Amara in escaping and, ultimately, put an end to Lilith's reign of terror. With each passing moment, my resolve grew stronger, and I knew that I would stop at nothing to secure our freedom.

* * *

Amara's recovery was slow yet consistent. With each passing day, she made progress in her movement and speech, gradually reclaiming her vigor and fortitude. This beacon of hope shone brightly amidst the oppressive despair of our confinement.

Weeks turned into a seemingly endless cycle of monotony and torture. Our bodies and spirits were battered and bruised, and our escape attempts seemed futile in the face of the reinforced door. Yet despite the overwhelming odds, we refused to give up. We made a promise to each other that we would never lose hope or abandon our love and trust for one another. It was our beacon of light in the darkest of times.

One unremarkable day, as we languished in our cramped quarters under the oppressive weight of our captivity, our ears were suddenly assaulted by the deafening sound of an explosion, followed by the cacophony of pirates screaming and writhing in agony. The force of the blast rocked our quarters, causing the walls to crumble and burst open, revealing two humanoid mercenary women standing in the rubble. The first was a breathtaking lynx girl with a bobbed mane of dark brown hair cascading over her shoulders, accentuating her striking features - piercing purple eyes, slightly dark skin, and big, brown black-tipped lynx ears. She wore a sleek, form-fitting suit adorned with white accents on the front and a purple turtleneck, while the back and sides were a deep, alluring purple.

A small lynx tail swished behind her, and a light brown satchel was wrapped around her waist, housing a sword in its holster. "The second was a lithe light-skinned cat girl with flowing black hair, razor-sharp pointy ears, yellow eyes, and a black choker studded with white spikes. She was dressed in a sleeveless black crop top, yellow finger less gloves, a black mini skirt with bold yellow stripes, black and yellow running shoes, and had a long, slender cat tail trailing behind her.

As soon as Amara caught sight of them, her eyes widened with excitement, and she exclaimed, "Ria and Cake!" These two skilled and experienced mercenaries were the ones Amara had signaled to our location with the tracker to rescue her from this forsaken slave ship.

I'm not going to lie; I wasn't sure if what I was seeing was real or just a hallucination caused by my prolonged thirst and hunger. Five pirates attempted to impede their progress. With lightning-fast reflexes, Ria dodged the pirates' clumsy strikes and swiftly struck back with her heavy sword, slicing through their defenses with ease. Meanwhile,

Cake's pistols barked out rounds, striking the pirates with deadly accuracy. The two yellow and black 9mm handguns glinted menacingly in the dim light, a testament to her skill as a sharpshooter.

Ria wasted no time in giving us clear instructions to stay close behind them. We hurriedly followed them out of the cramped quarters, feeling a sense of relief and hope wash over us as we made our way to the deck. I could hear the sound of bullets whizzing by us, but Ria was quick to defend us. With her swords in hand, she skillfully deflected the bullets away from us, creating a barrier of steel around us. Meanwhile, Cake was busy unleashing a barrage of bullets from her pistols, taking down pirates left and right.

When we reached the deck, the situation was chaotic. Pirates were everywhere, and they were armed to the teeth. But that didn't seem to faze Ria and Cake. They worked together in perfect harmony, Ria using her swords to slice through the waves of attackers while Cake used her pistols to take out anyone who got too close.

Their moves were swift and precise, and it was clear that they were highly trained professionals. The pirates didn't stand a chance against them. I stood back, in awe of their skills, as they took down hordes of attackers with ease. It was like watching a deadly dance, with each move perfectly choreographed.

As the pirates continued to pour out onto the deck, Ria and Cake were starting to get outnumbered. That's when Ria turned to us and yelled, "Amara and you, jump out and swim to the bi-plane! We'll meet you there!"

I was hesitant to leave their side, but I knew that we had to trust them.

Without a second thought, Amara and I jumped off the ship and into the water. We swam as fast as we could towards the bi-plane, feeling the bullets whiz by us.

    Finally, we reached the plane and climbed aboard, gasping for air. We looked out to see Ria and Cake still fighting off the pirates on the ship. I felt a surge of gratitude toward them for saving us. Cake pulled out a small bag of mini explosives from her pocket and swiftly tossed them at a group of pirates, taking them out in a deafening blast of smoke and fire. The pirates scattered and regrouped, but Ria and Cake were relentless, striking them down with grace and force. Despite being outnumbered, the two mercenaries held their ground, taking out pirates from every direction.

Observing from the secure confines of the biplane, a sense of both admiration and apprehension swept over me as I watched their abilities unfold. They exhibited a natural aptitude for combat, each movement executed with flawless fluidity and precision. I couldn't help but wonder how many conflicts they had faced before.

* * *

After what seemed like an eternity, the last of the pirates fell, and Ria and Cake stood victorious on the deck of the ship. But their triumph was short-lived as the never-before-seen captain emerged from the chaos with more pirates. He was a towering figure with bulging muscles and a fierce scowl, bellowing a challenge at Ria and Cake. The two women met him head-on.

Ria's swords sang through the air as they clashed against the captain's massive cutlass, sending sparks flying with each strike. Despite Ria's skill, the captain's brute strength was too much to handle. He swung his weapon with a fierce intensity that forced Ria on the defensive.

Meanwhile, Cake kept her wits about her as she took out pirates with her explosives. She quickly noticed some pirates attempting to flank Ria and sprang into action. With a flick of her wrist, she tossed a bomb their way, sending them flying. She then turned her attention to help Ria, dodging and weaving through the chaos to get to her side.

Ria and Cake fought back with renewed determination, now working together again in perfect harmony. Ria's precise strikes found their mark, while Cake's explosive attacks held the pirates at bay. The captain, who had previously been confident in his abilities, now found himself struggling to keep up with their coordinated assault. His blows landed with diminishing force, and exhaustion began to take its toll.

As the fierce battle raged on, I stood at the edge of my seat, my heart racing with anticipation, silently rooting for Ria and Cake to emerge victorious.
   The atmosphere was charged with tension, and the sound of metal clashing against metal echoed through the air. With each passing moment, the captain's muscles seemed to bulge with even more ferocity, unleashing a relentless barrage of attacks against Ria and Cake. His blows were so devastating that they shook the ship to its core, and I feared for the safety of everyone on board. Despite their valiant efforts, Ria and Cake were unable to avoid taking serious hits, and both sides were drawing blood in this fierce battle for survival.

As the grueling battle persisted, the mercenaries grew increasingly fatigued, their stamina dwindling with every passing moment. Meanwhile, the captain only seemed to be getting stronger, cackling and mocking them as he dealt merciless blows that left them reeling. The odds were decidedly not in favor of Ria and Cake, and victory seemed impossible.

Just as the captain was about to strike the final blow, the sound of a gunshot pierced the air. A fresh, clean bullet wound appeared in his head, and the captain fell to the ground lifeless. It was Amara who fired the shot, her expression stern and focused as she held a vintage revolver with fresh smoke coming out of the barrel. Cake couldn't resist making a joke, remarking that Amara had finally decided to find her gun. Both Ria and Cake laughed, the relief of victory washing over them.

Ria and Cake took a moment to catch their breath, their laughter slowly subsiding as they regained their composure. They got up, brushing off their clothes and popping some bones back into place. Despite the bruises and cuts that covered their bodies, they were both still smiling. They had faced incredible odds and come out victorious, and that feeling of triumph was hard to beat.

* * *

As the remaining pirates turned and fled in fear, I couldn't help but feel grateful to Ria and Cake for risking their lives to save us. I knew that I owed them a debt that I could never repay. Despite being bruised and battered, Ria and Cake swam back to the biplane and took their positions at the controls, thanking Amara for saving them. In turn, Amara expressed her gratitude towards our rescuers for saving our lives and safeguarding her prized revolver.

Ria reached into the plane's dashboard, grabbed a can labeled "Rapid-Heal," and swiftly sprayed it on themselves. The injuries disappeared as

Chapter 4 "The Mercenaries Tail"

if by magic. They turned to me and asked if we needed help. I gestured towards Amara's back, where a partially healed bullet wound remained. Ria handled the wound with the skill of a seasoned nurse, removing the bullet fragments and using the spray to heal Amara's injury. With Cake's exceptional piloting skills, we set a course toward our path to freedom.

As we soared into the sky, I couldn't help but feel grateful for the two extraordinary women beside me. Their heroic actions would forever be etched in my mind, and I knew that I would never forget them.

In the glow of the slave ship's fiery demise, Amara had succumbed to exhaustion and fallen asleep. Ria and Cake bombarded me with questions about my story, eager to know more about my experiences and how I had ended up in captivity.

At first, I hesitated to share, not wanting to relive the trauma of my captivity, but their persistence made me realize that sharing my story might help me heal. As I recounted my tale, starting with my first love, Lilith, who turned out to be a serial killer, Ria, and Cake listened with empathy and understanding. They shared their own experiences as mercenaries, regaling me with tales of their adventures and close calls.

Ria exuded a serious sense of leadership, while Cake constantly lightened the mood with her humor, even making Ria laugh. Their close relationship was evident, but I didn't want to pry by asking if they were a couple.

* * *

After some time, Amara woke up and expressed her curiosity about how they were able to find them, considering her tracker had malfunctioned. Ria then proceeded to recount the process of tracking them down, using Amara's malfunctioning tracker. "It was a bit of a challenge, but not impossible," Ria explained. "I analyzed the last signal the tracker emitted and its trajectory. With a combination of logical deduction and intuition, I was eventually able to locate you guys. Sorry, it took so long."

"It's okay, by the way, do you still have my old stash of trackers?" Amara asked.

Ria rummaged through the plane's dashboard and produced a bag of small white and silver dots. "Ah, here it is," Ria said, handing it to Amara.

Amara expressed gratitude and started tinkering with the trackers. "Thank you. But next time, you should hide my gun as well as these trackers. It took me ages to steal it, and I'd be devastated if I lost it," she joked.

Ria apologized for how they hid the gun but then teased Amara about taking so long to shoot the captain. Amara admitted, "To be honest, I was rusty. It's been a while since I've fired a gun, so it was a lucky shot."

Ria chuckled and teased Amara, "Since when do you get rusty? You should stick with us again. You never get rusty or caught for that matter." Amara smiled but shook her head. "You know I like doing my own thing."

Ria then asked, "I know you're a first-class thief and all, but it's not like you to get captured. What happened back there?" Amara looked away for a moment before answering, "It was a trap. I let my guard down and got careless." Ria retorted, "You get caught? No way." She then asked, "Are you alright?" Amara glanced at me out of the corner of her eye before responding, "Yeah, I'm fine." A smile spread across her face. "Well, I'm grateful that you guys were able to rescue me."

Ria shrugged nonchalantly and replied, "We're just returning the favor for all the times you've bailed us out, like that time during the jewel heist when Cake got stuck in a high-security vault with lasers, electrified floors, walls, and flamethrowers."

Cake shuddered as she gazed into the distance, a haunted expression crossing her face. "The burning...," she whispered, lost in thought.

Ria placed a hand on Cake's shoulder, bringing her back to the present. "But besides that, we genuinely enjoy your company, Amara," she said with a smile.

Amara's face lit up with gratitude. "Thank you, Ria. I've enjoyed being with you both as well."

Cake chimed in, a mischievous glint in her eye. "Yeah, and let's not forget how much fun we have with you around, Amara. You always bring excitement and adventure to the table. Who knows what kind of trouble we'll get into next!"

As the trio talked, I gradually drifted off to sleep, feeling a comforting presence snuggle up to me. At first, I thought I was imagining it, but then a warm, big, soft tail wrapped around me, and arms enveloped me in a warm embrace. A head rested on mine, and the soothing warmth lulled me into a peaceful slumber. Before I fully succumbed to sleep,

I briefly wondered who it was, but the comforting embrace was all I needed to let go of all my worries.

Chapter 5 "A Long Way From Home"

In the dream, I woke up in a daze, disoriented and confused. The last thing I remembered was Lilith holding me at gunpoint. But now, I found myself in an alleyway, with no idea how I had gotten there. Lilith was still there, her tear-streaked face now a blur as she ordered me to leave. I stumbled away from her, trying to make sense of what had just happened.

However, my confusion quickly turned to horror as Lilith suddenly lunged at me, her teeth bared and ready to sink into my flesh. I screamed in terror as she tore into me, her apologies mingling with the sounds of her chewing. Suddenly, out of nowhere, the silhouette of Amara emerged from the shadows. Lilith stopped her attack, visibly terrified at the sight of Amara. I watched in shock as they faced off, their eyes locked in a silent battle of wills.

And then, just as suddenly as it had begun, the dream abruptly ended, and I found myself back in the real world. The sound of the plane sputtering and shaking brought me back to reality, and I realized that

Ria and Cake were frantically trying to diagnose the problem. Ria leaned over the dashboard, inspecting the propellers with a concerned look on her face.

"We need to find a place to land. The propellers need repairs," she said, her voice urgent.

Ria scanned the horizon, searching for a safe place to touch down. Her eyes eventually landed on a small island in the distance.

"That's our best option. We can land there and hopefully find the supplies we need to fix the plane," she said, pointing towards the island.

With Cake's expert piloting, we managed to navigate through the rough terrain and land safely on the island. The plane shuddered and shook on impact, but we were all relieved to be on solid ground.

After safely landing the plane, Ria and Cake got to work assessing the damage and collecting the necessary supplies. Despite my eagerness to help, they insisted that I rest and recover from the harrowing experience. Amara and I sat together, chatting and reminiscing about the recent events on the slave ship.

A mix of relief and anxiety washed over me as I considered our situation. We had managed to escape the slave ship, but the journey back home was far from certain. Amara, whom I had taken care of while she was injured, expressed her regret for not thanking me earlier. Her words warmed my heart, but I couldn't help feeling weighed down by memories of Lilith. Amara then revealed that she remembered the moment when I had confessed my love to her while I held her injured body, and all the emotions of that memory came flooding back.

Suddenly, Amara leaned in to kiss me and pleaded with me to stay with her. Though her sadness and disappointment were palpable when I pulled away, I knew that I couldn't ignore my own conflicted feelings. "I'm sorry if I gave you the wrong idea," I told her. "But I'm not emotionally available at the moment. However, I do care for you deeply." Although she nodded and said she understood, her face betrayed her true feelings, and I couldn't help but feel terrible.

* * *

Later, when we discussed the logistics of my journey, Ria informed me that reaching New Colombia by plane was not an option due to the need for refueling. Navigating the uncharted seas by boat would also be treacherous, leaving an airship as the best option. However, they were rare and typically reserved for military or commercial liners. The realization hit me hard - I might not make it back home.

Ria and Cake noticed my distress and empathized with my predicament. While Ria shared a few ideas, Cake appeared to disagree, and they exchanged a few words about possible solutions.

After some contemplation, Ria approached me tentatively with a suggestion. "I know it's not ideal, but there's a chance we might be able to find an airship at a nearby island military trading post. However, I have to warn you, it won't be easy. The place is heavily guarded, and the risk of getting caught is high," she said, her voice unsure.

Although the thought of returning home was exciting, the idea of stealing made me uneasy. Cake shared her concerns too, emphasizing that they were mercenaries and needed compensation for their help.

"As much as we want to assist you, we have to earn a living, and this is not going to be an easy task. We can't do this without proper compensation," Cake apologized.

Ria reluctantly agreed, citing the potential consequences of stealing from such an outpost. "I understand how difficult this situation is for you, but we have to be careful. Getting caught could have severe implications for us," she said, her expression grave.

Amara offered her skills as a thief, but she knew that she couldn't do it alone. She tried to convince Ria and Cake to lend a hand, even if it was just a small one.

"I know we can't expect you to work for free," Amara said with a sincere tone, "but any assistance would be greatly appreciated. I promise to make it worth your while." She placed a hand on my shoulder as if to emphasize her plea.

Ria glanced down at Amara's hand resting on my shoulder and offered a small smile. She then turned to Cake and began discussing the situation further.

"We'll help you, but we'll need your help too, Jon," Ria said, her voice firm.

Chapter 5 "A Long Way From Home"

* * *

As I watched Ria put the finishing touches on the plane's repairs, Cake and Amara huddled together, discussing their plan to steal the airship. I knew that I needed to get back home as soon as possible, but the plan sounded risky, and I didn't want to endanger anyone.

Cake explained the plan in a low voice, "We'll need to wait until nightfall when the guards are changing shifts, and we'll need to be quick. We can't risk getting caught."

Amara nodded in agreement, "And we'll need to disable the security systems if we want any chance of getting in undetected."

Ria added her concerns, "And what about the guards inside the trading post? We'll need to neutralize them too."

Cake assured her, "I have some experience with that kind of thing. We'll need to gather some equipment, though."

I hesitated and asked, "Are you sure you guys want to do this?"

Amara placed a comforting hand on my shoulder, "We have to do whatever it takes to get you home, Jon. We'll make sure to keep you safe."

Ria and Cake nodded in agreement, their expressions determined, "We've got your back," Ria said.

I took a deep breath and prepared myself for the mission ahead. With the four of us together, we set off toward the trading post, determined to put our plan into action. Even though I felt a sense of apprehension, I also felt a glimmer of hope that I would soon be back home and be able to stop Lilith.

* * *

While flying towards the island where the military trading post was located, a brewing storm caused the wind to howl, and the plane shook violently, making me grip my seat tightly in fear as thunder illuminated the dark sky, revealing ominous clouds that surrounded us.

Ria's voice came through the turbulence, trying to reassure us. "We'll make it through this. The plane is built to withstand these kinds of conditions."

Cake nodded, her eyes focused on the controls in front of her. "I'll do my best to keep us steady," she said, her voice laced with determination.

As we continued flying through the storm, a sudden gust of wind hit the plane, causing it to lurch to the side. I let out a gasp of fear as my anxiety skyrocketed. However, Amara's reassuring hand landed on my arm. "It's okay," she said, her voice steady. "We're going to make it through this."

I nodded, trying to calm my racing heart. Despite the chaos outside, I felt a sense of safety. As the storm raged on, we continued to fly towards the military trading post, our destination still in sight despite the turbulent conditions. I closed my eyes, trying to relax and trust in the skills of our pilots.

As soon as I opened my eyes again, the lightning storm intensified, illuminating the dark sky with bright flashes of light. The rain pounded against the plane, reducing visibility. The plane shook violently as we passed through a thick cloud, and we were suddenly plunged into complete darkness. The turbulence got worse, and the lightning flashes illuminated the cockpit, casting eerie shadows on the pilots' faces.

"I can barely see anything," Cake shouted over the noise of the storm.

"We have to keep going," Ria yelled back. "We can't turn back now."

The lightning flashed around them, illuminating the dark clouds for just a moment before plunging them back into darkness. I couldn't help but feel a sense of dread as the storm raged on, wondering if we would make it through.

Suddenly, there was a blinding flash of light, and a loud crackling sound filled the air. A bolt of lightning had struck the biplane, ripping off a large piece of the plane's wing and causing it to spin out of control.

I remember feeling weightless for a moment as the plane plummeted toward the ocean below. Then everything went black

* * *

When I opened my eyes, a surge of panic flooded my senses as I realized I was submerged in the water. Waves crashed around me, tossing me to and fro like a ragdoll. My head throbbed with pain, and I struggled to stay conscious as I gasped for air. In the distance, I could make out the wreckage of a biplane and a thick plume of smoke trailing over the horizon. With every passing second, it became more difficult to stay afloat. My limbs felt like lead, and my movements slowed. I knew I had to find safety soon, or else I would be consumed by the unforgiving ocean. As I fought to keep my head above water, I spotted a piece of wreckage floating nearby. Summoning all the strength I had left, I managed to haul myself onto it. However, my body was wracked with pain, and I blacked out again as I lay there, stranded in the vast expanse of the ocean.

Chapter 6 "The Abandoned City"

Slowly, I regained consciousness with the taste of salt still lingering on my lips. Blinking, I shook my head in an attempt to clear the fog in my mind. I gasped when I realized that I was no longer in the water, but instead lying on a sandy beach surrounded by debris from various wrecks, including a biplane that resembled the one we had been traveling in. A sinking feeling washed over me as I scanned the beach, finding no sign of Ria, Cake, or Amara.

As I sat up slowly, a wave of dizziness washed over me. My head was pounding, and I felt a sharp pain in my side. My clothes were soaked through, and I shivered as a cold wind blew through the beach. However, when I tried to stand up, my legs felt weak and unsteady, causing me to stumble forward a few steps before collapsing onto the sand. The island seemed deserted with no signs of civilization.

It was clear that I was in no shape to go anywhere or do anything. I needed to rest and recover. As I lay there staring at the clear blue sky above, a sense of despair crept in. I was stranded on an unknown island, injured, and without any way to contact anyone for help. However, I refused to give up hope, knowing that Ria, Cake, and Amara were out there somewhere, and I had to believe that they were still alive.

With that thought in mind, I closed my eyes and tried to rest, hoping that help would arrive soon. Time seemed to pass slowly, and my thoughts drifted to memories of our journey so far. I began to wonder if people had been killed trying to help me due to my bad decision not to contact the proper authorities about Lilith because I was too "depressed" to do so. However, I refused to let negative thoughts take over. I knew that I needed to stay positive and focused, no matter how dire the situation appeared.

Eventually, I drifted off to sleep, my body exhausted and my mind overwhelmed. The sound of waves crashing against the shore and seagulls chirping in the distance lulled me into a deep slumber. When I woke up, the sun was setting on the horizon, casting a warm glow on the beach. I felt a sense of calm wash over me, knowing that I had survived another day. I closed my eyes again and dozed off.

***

The next morning, I woke up with a pounding headache and my body aching all over from the crash. Despite the pain, I knew that finding water and food was essential to my survival. So, I slowly got to my feet and stumbled into the forest, trying to get my bearings.

As I walked through the dense foliage, my eyes scanned the area for any signs of water or food. The trees loomed above me, their branches

Chapter 6 "The Abandoned City"

twisting and reaching toward the sky. Suddenly, my foot caught on a hidden rock, and I stumbled forward, tumbling down a steep cliffside.

I landed with a splash in a pond, and the cold water jolted me awake. I shook my head to clear the dizziness and struggled to my feet, shivering from the chill. I took a moment to brush the dirt and leaves off my clothes, and as I looked up, I saw something that made me stop in my tracks.

A massive abandoned city stretched out before me, with buildings towering over the landscape in various states of decay and ruin. Nature had reclaimed the area, with vines and weeds snaking their way up the sides of the crumbling structures. Abandoned cars littered the streets, rusted, and left behind as if their owners had fled in a hurry.

I tried to stay focused on my mission to find water and food, but my mind couldn't help but wander to thoughts of what had happened here. Where had everyone gone? What had caused such destruction? I continued walking, my footsteps echoing in the silence. I came across a few shops, their windows shattered and shelves stripped bare. I searched through them, hoping to find something to eat or drink, but they were all empty.

✳ ✳ ✳

After wandering through the abandoned city for what seemed like an eternity, I finally stumbled upon a room that seemed promising. It had a sink and some cabinets, giving me hope that I might find some much-needed supplies. I walked over to the sink and turned on the tap, half-expecting nothing to happen. To my surprise, the tap worked, but the water that came out was dirty and brown.

I knew I couldn't drink the water like that, so I began to search the cabinets for any tools or supplies that could help me purify it. After a few minutes of searching, I found a small pan and a box of matches. A little bit of hope sparked within me as I realized that I might be able to make the water safe to drink.

I filled the pan with water from the sink and set it on a nearby stove. Using the matches, I lit a small flame beneath the pan and waited patiently for the water to come to a boil. As I watched the water heat up, I couldn't help but feel grateful for the simple tools that I had found. In a world that had been destroyed by some unknown catastrophe, even the most basic supplies felt like a lifeline.

After a few minutes, the water finally began to boil, and I carefully removed the pan from the stove. I waited for it to cool down a bit before tentatively taking a sip. It wasn't the best-tasting water I'd ever had, but it was clean and safe to drink, which was all that mattered.

Feeling slightly more refreshed and energized, I decided to continue my exploration of the city, hoping to find more supplies and perhaps some clues about what had happened to this once-thriving place. As I aimlessly wandered through the abandoned city, the vast emptiness and eerie silence left me feeling overwhelmingly lonely. My mind fixated on the fate of my dear friends, Amara, Ria, and Cake. My heart ached with uncertainty: were they still alive? Had they managed to escape the catastrophic plane crash and ensuing storm to find safety? These thoughts weighed heavily on me as I scoured the city for any basic necessities I could find.

Chapter 6 "The Abandoned City"

* * *

After what felt like hours of rummaging through various buildings, my stomach grumbled with hunger. Finally, I stumbled upon a stash of canned food. The cans were rusted and dented, and their contents looked unappetizing at best. But I was determined to make the most of my situation. Armed with my trusty match-and-pan combo, I mixed all the canned goods together and cooked them over an open flame until they were somewhat edible. The smell was nauseating, but I forced myself to take a bite. The taste was even worse than I had anticipated - metallic and sour, with an aftertaste that lingered on my tongue. I knew I probably shouldn't eat it, but beggars can't be choosers. Unfortunately, my triumph was short-lived as the unpalatable meal left me feeling ill and desperate for relief.

As I scoured the area for a place to rest, my legs heavy and aching, I finally came across an abandoned building with a queen-size bed. The sight of such comfort amid the decay of the city was both strange and surreal. I sank into the soft mattress, the linens smelling musty and damp. Despite the relief of a soft bed, sleep did not come easily to me. Every creak of the building and rustle of the wind outside made me feel more uneasy.

The darkness of the room was oppressive, and I could barely make out the outlines of abandoned furniture and debris littering the floor. The silence was broken only by the sound of my breathing, which seemed unnaturally loud in the stillness of the room. I wrapped myself tightly in the thin blanket, feeling as though I was trying to shield myself from an unknown danger lurking in the shadows.

In the dead of night, a terrifying nightmare jolted me awake. In my dream, Lilith had found me and was relentlessly pursuing me with her cold, reddish-pink eyes. I could feel her icy breath on my neck as she whispered, "I found you." My heart raced as I frantically tried to escape her grasp. When I woke up, my sheets were soaked with sweat, and I couldn't shake the feeling of impending danger that still lingered in my mind.

I tried once again to get some rest, hoping for a peaceful night's sleep. As I drifted off, I found myself in a dream where Amara was the star. She was twirling and laughing in a field of vibrant wildflowers, and her infectious smile filled me with warmth. I longed to join her in her dance, but the weight of my worries held me back.

Despite my hesitation, Amara took my hand and pulled me into the dance. We spun and twirled together, weightless and free from the burdens of reality. The sun beamed down on us, and the gentle breeze carried the sweet fragrance of blooming flowers. Everything felt perfect at that moment, yet my heart couldn't shake the thought of Lilith, leaving me with a bittersweet feeling.

Suddenly, the dream began to shift, and the idyllic scene started to twist and warp. Then the sky darkened, and the flowers wilted and withered. Amara's expression changed from joy to fear, and she started to back away from me.

Before I could react, a shadowy figure emerged from the darkness, and I recognized it as Lilith. She was laughing, her eyes flashing with madness, as she reached for me. I tried to run, but my feet felt like they were stuck in molasses, and I couldn't escape her grasp.

Chapter 6 "The Abandoned City"

Just as Lilith's hands closed around my throat, I jolted awake, gasping for air. The relief of waking up from that nightmare was overwhelming, and I sat there for a few moments, catching my breath and trying to shake off the lingering fear.

Despite the terrifying end to the dream, I couldn't help but feel grateful for the moments of peace and happiness that I had experienced with Amara.

* * *

The next morning, I woke up with a renewed sense of determination to find my companions and leave the island. After hours of searching, I stumbled upon a surprising discovery - a derelict arcade. Despite its neglected appearance, the arcade machines were well-preserved and sparked my curiosity. As I delved deeper, I stumbled upon a cache of old military equipment hidden behind the counter. Although I was unable to recognize its military origin, a note inscribed in a strange language caught my attention, resembling Lilith's handwriting. However, I dismissed it as a mere coincidence and continued to explore.

As I ventured further into the arcade, I came across a generator room with an old-looking generator that had a lever. Though hesitant at first, I gave in to my curiosity and pulled the lever, causing all the machines and lights to come to life, creating a mesmerizing light show. Despite knowing that I shouldn't waste my time, I couldn't resist the temptation to play video games. It had been months since I last played, and I needed a reprieve from all the despair. In a moment of weakness, I spent hours engrossed in the games, losing track of time and the outside world. One thing I noticed was the initials "Lil" on the high scoreboard.

The hours I spent playing video games in the arcade turned into a full day. As the sun began to set, I realized how much time had passed and that I needed to continue my search for my friends. With a heavy heart, I left the arcade, feeling a tinge of guilt for wasting so much time but it felt so good at the moment.

I soon realized that I had made no progress in my search. Exhausted and hungry, I decided to take a rest for the night feeling extremely guilty for the way I spent my time. I found a small apartment overlooking the arcade with a sofa bed and decided to stay there for the night. As I lay in bed, my mind was consumed with thoughts of my friends, Amara, Ria, and Cake. I couldn't shake the feeling that they were out there somewhere, waiting for me to find them. Despite my exhaustion, I forced myself to stay awake, brainstorming possible leads and ways to track them down.

Eventually, the weariness of the day caught up with me, and I drifted off into a restless sleep. In my dreams, I found myself wandering through a maze of dark corridors and hidden passageways, searching for any sign of my missing companions. The dream felt so vivid and real that I could almost taste the salt air and feel the gritty sand beneath my feet. But then, as I turned a corner, I heard Lilith's voice echoing through the maze, screaming for me. Panic flooded my body as I realized she was giving chase. I ran as fast as I could, but the corridors seemed to stretch on forever, and every turn led me deeper into the labyrinth. The sound of Lilith's laughter and the scrape of her knife against the walls filled my ears, driving me to the brink of madness.

I jolted awake, my heart racing, startled by a deafening explosion that shook the building. Quickly, I realized it had come from outside and leaped out of bed to investigate. Rushing to the window, I peered out

Chapter 6 "The Abandoned City"

and was met with a horrifying sight. The once-pristine arcade I had explored just the day before was now engulfed in a massive fireball, flames reaching up into the sky. I wondered what could have caused the explosion, and my mind immediately went to the generator I had used to power the arcade. Looking at the thick smoke rising into the sky, an idea struck me. The smoke could serve as a signal, attracting the attention of anyone passing by.

Without hesitation, I set to work, gathering as much dry brush and debris as I could find in the surrounding area. Carefully piling it up in a large heap near the burning arcade, I made sure to create as much smoke and flames as possible. Watching the fire grow, I couldn't help but feel a sense of hope. Maybe someone would see the smoke and come to investigate.

But as the flames died down and the smoke began to dissipate, I realized that my hopes may have been in vain. The island seemed as deserted as ever, but I wasn't giving up. Searching for anything that could help me start a fire, my eyes scanned the abandoned buildings, looking for any potential sources of fuel. Finally, I stumbled upon an old supermarket, and my heart leaped with excitement. Inside, I found stacks of cardboard boxes, piles of newspapers, and even some old gasoline cans.

With trembling hands, I gathered the materials and began to pile them up in a corner of the store. Feeling the heat radiating off the pile, I struck a match and held it to the paper. Suddenly, the pile erupted in flames, and I stepped back, watching as the fire grew higher and higher. The flames danced and crackled, casting eerie shadows on the walls around me. Feeling a sense of satisfaction, I watched the smoke rise into the sky. Maybe someone would see it and come to my rescue, or maybe my friends would see it and know that I was still alive, still searching for them.

As the fire burned on, I sat down and watched it, lost in thought. Even as I tried to find hope in the flames, I couldn't shake the feeling of despair that lingered in my heart. Would I ever find my friends? Or was I doomed to wander this desolate island alone?

After setting the fire earlier, I searched for a new building to sleep in. Eventually, I found a spot near a window where I could rest. As exhaustion overtook me, I drifted off to sleep. However, I was abruptly awakened by the sound of large footsteps vibrating through the ground. The rumbling stopped, and an eerie silence filled the air. Instinctively, I remained completely still, feeling like something was watching me. Slowly, I turned towards the window only to see a giant reddish-pink eye staring directly at me, sending chills through my body.

my heart was pounding in my chest as I slowly climbed out of bed, my body drenched in sweat. Suddenly, a loud crash startled me, and I turned to see a large hole in the wall, revealing a pale hand reaching for me. Without thinking, I sprinted away as fast as I could, the hand continuing to smash through the walls behind me as I ran down the dark hallway. The sound of my footsteps echoed off the walls, and I could feel my heart pounding harder and harder with each passing second.

As I reached the end of the corridor, I saw an opportunity and leaped from a nearby window. The rush of wind filled my ears as I fell four stories down, landing in a nearby dumpster with a loud thud. I gasped for air, trying to catch my breath, and looked around for any sign of the creature that was giving chase.

Chapter 6 "The Abandoned City"

Suddenly, the pale hand attempted to smash the dumpster, and I jumped out just in time, running out of the alley and into the street. I could feel the adrenaline coursing through my veins as I ran, trying to put as much distance as possible between me and the creature,

  I could hear the creature still in pursuit, its relentless chasing driving me forward. With my heart pounding in my chest, I ran as fast as I could, determined to stay ahead of the creature's grasp. Despite the fear consuming me, I knew I couldn't give up. I had to keep fighting for my life, no matter what.

* * *

I had been chased for hours throughout the abandoned city by the creature, its giant pale hand reaching out for me at every turn as it smashed through walls and obstacles behind me. I ran through narrow alleyways, from one building to the next, hoping to find a way out. But it seemed like I was cornered with no escape. The creature loomed over me, taking advantage of my vulnerability. But I refused to give in without a struggle. As it reached down towards me, I quickly scanned my surroundings for an escape. That's when I spotted a nearby window, and without hesitation, I grabbed a brick and smashed it open. With adrenaline coursing through my veins, I leaped through the shattered glass and landed inside.

Heart racing, I made a run for the building's exit, frantically searching for a place to hide. The creature's footsteps echoed behind me, urging me to move faster. Every turn felt like a dead end until I spotted a small alcove that seemed to offer some cover. I dove inside and tried to control my breathing as I listened for any sign of the creature's approach.

As the creature's footsteps drew nearer, I sprang out of the alcove, my heart pounding in my chest. My eyes frantically scanned the area for a safe haven, finally landing on an abandoned car dealership nearby. Without hesitation, I bolted towards it, desperate for cover. Reaching the back of the building, I searched for a suitable hiding spot and my gaze settled on a black SUV with its driver-side window rolled down.

Without wasting any time, I deftly crawled through the window and attempted to inch my way further back to conceal myself. However, my shirt got snagged on the handbrake, and in my panic, I unintentionally released it. The car suddenly lurched out of park, throwing me into the backseat and sending the vehicle hurtling down the incline of the dealership.

As the car gained momentum, I realized that I had to act quickly to prevent a catastrophic accident. However, my attempts to stop the car proved futile as it picked up speed, crashing through a side window and careening down the slope, wreaking havoc along its path. Mailboxes, parking meters, and small trees were no match for the runaway vehicle.

My heart raced as I frantically searched for a way to stop the car, but it was too late. The sound of crashing metal echoed in my ears as the car careened down the hill, leaving a trail of destruction in its wake. Finally, the car came to a stop by crashing into a storefront with a loud crash, drawing attention to my location.

Chapter 6 "The Abandoned City"

Chapter 7 "Cosmic Despair"

As I climbed out of the car, I felt the pain of the crash coursing through my body. My vision was blurry as I stumbled away from the wreckage, but something caught my attention. A giant figure, at least 80 ft tall, loomed over me, its form obscured by the sun. My anxiety rose as I froze in place, unable to move, as a pale hand reached down towards me, grabbing me by the waist and lifting me up towards its face.

As I focused my gaze on the figure holding me, I immediately recognized her as Lilith. However, her appearance was noticeably different. While her signature white hair and striking pinkish-red eyes remained unchanged, her long rabbit ears hung limply behind her head, in stark contrast to Lilith's usually perky stance. To add to her unexpected appearance, she was clad in a well-worn, silver space suit that hugged her form snugly. The suit had a turtleneck, and its metallic sheen indicated that it had seen its fair share of wear and tear. Nevertheless, it fit her comfortably, as if it were a second skin. She also wore two bulky black bracelets.

Chapter 7 "Cosmic Despair"

I was left speechless, stunned by the sight before me. The woman, who resembled Lilith (or was it Her?), sniffed me with a smirk on her face, slowly opening her mouth and pushing me towards it. My eyes widened in terror as I gazed into her gaping maw, knowing that I was about to be devoured. I desperately kicked off one of my shoes, which landed on her tongue, but she simply tossed it back into her throat with her tongue and continued to lower me in with a sickeningly playful demeanor. The mere sight of her mouth, dripping with saliva and smelling of decay, made me feel queasy.

In my desperation, I let out a bloodcurdling scream. "Please, don't do this, Lilith!" The giant's grip on me momentarily paused as she held me up to her face. Her expression shifted from one of disturbing glee to that of confusion. Her voice trembling with curiosity, she asked, "Lilith? Why did you call me Lilith?"

My response came out in a terrified and shaky voice, "You're not Lilith."

At that moment, the giant experienced an epiphany. Her eyes widened with realization as she spoke, "My name is Lila, but I do have a sister named Lilith who looks just like me. Do you happen to know her?"

As the giant tightened her grip around me, my heart pounded in my chest. I couldn't believe what I was seeing - a being that bore an exact resemblance to Lilith but towered over me at an impossible height. It was a living nightmare. My voice quivered with nerves as I struggled to process the gravity of the situation. "Y-yes, she was my girlfriend," I managed to stammer out. The giant's massive face drew nearer to mine, her gaze scrutinizing me with a curious expression.

As I met Lila's gaze, I couldn't help but notice a glimmer of curiosity in her eyes, albeit tainted with a hint of disdain toward me. "How is she?" she inquired, the inflection in her voice hinting at genuine concern for her sister Lilith's well-being.

After a brief pause, I found myself fabricating a response: "Uh, she's doing well."

To my surprise, Lila was taken aback by my response. "Why would Lilith involve herself with food?" she sneered, her disgust evident.

I felt a chill run down my spine at her words, realizing that Lila had no qualms about eating humans. "What do you mean by that?" I asked, my fear starting to turn into anger.

Lila then disclosed a shocking truth: both she and Lilith were extraterrestrial beings from a planet that invaded this region two decades ago to exploit its natural resources. After the majority of their troops were defeated or fled, the two of them remained stranded on this island, fearing punishment for their inability to complete the mission.

As fugitives, they subsisted on a vegetarian diet for a decade, concealing themselves in the woods. However, Lila and Lilith's survival became jeopardized as the local vegetation could not sustain them anymore. Consequently, they turned to hunting animals for nourishment. But the taste of human flesh proved too irresistible after two unfortunate humans stumbled upon them in the woods. From then on, their appetite for human meat became insatiable, leading them to terrorize the island's inhabitants.

The island's government threw everything it had at Lila and Lilith to stop them. However, faced with the threat to their food source, the two had no choice but to fight back. Lilith ingeniously created bracelets using leftover spaceship fuel and spaceship parts, which granted them near-invincibility. These bracelets enabled them to remain untouchable for years, allowing them to abduct people at will and come and go as they pleased in the city.

One fateful day, a mysterious plague swept through the island, devastating both human and animal populations. Lila and Lilith were left without a reliable source of sustenance. Lila suspected that the outbreak was the result of a scientist's desperate attempt to stop them, but the plan had backfired.

Determined to ensure their survival, Lila embarked on a daunting task. She scoured the island for rare spaceship engine parts and special emergency spaceship fuel, which she used to create a device capable of shrinking them down to human size. With this device, they could leave and live amongst human society. After months of toiling away, the device was finally ready for testing.

Lila decided to test the device on her sister, Lilith. To their amazement, the experiment was a success. Lilith was reduced to human size, but the machine had sustained irreparable damage. In a selfless act, Lila fashioned a boat out of salvaged military parts and sent Lilith off into the unknown, bidding her farewell with a heavy heart. Lila hoped that her sister would find a better life and survive, even if it meant sacrificing her chance at survival.

Soon, Lilith realized that the use of the machine had an unexpected side effect, creating unpredictable weather patterns that caused frequent shipwrecks and plane crashes. These accidents drew survivors to the island, providing Lilith with a persistent food source. She was now filled with regret for sending her sister away, especially now that she had a consistent source of food again.

This shed new light on Lilith's actions and helped me understand, but not fully, the reasons behind her heinous acts. In retrospect, it was evident that she was plagued with an insatiable hunger for human flesh, which she fought against with all her might. However, her willpower ultimately gave in to the overwhelming desire, leading her down a dark path and into a state of despair. It was a heartbreaking realization, and I couldn't help but feel a twinge of sympathy for her plight.

I struggled to comprehend Lilith's continued consumption of humans, considering she is a talented inventor. I couldn't help but blurt out, "But why humans? There has to be a better way than cannibalism?"

Lilith's expression turned cold and condescending as she retorted, "Don't you think I've considered a better solution for food? And as for cannibalism, humans consume meat, so what makes it any different?"

I was stunned by Lilith's dismissive response. "But we're sentient beings, capable of reason and empathy. It's wrong to eat each other," I insisted.

Lilith's cold expression and her tone remained the same. "You humans have a narrow view of the world. From our perspective, eating other sentient beings is no different from eating any other animal. And besides, we're not even the same race," she retorted.

I struggled to comprehend her twisted logic and lack of empathy. How could she be so indifferent to the suffering of others?

Chapter 7 "Cosmic Despair"

I desperately tried to reason with her, to make her see the immorality of consuming sentient beings. But her warped logic and utter lack of empathy convinced me that she was beyond reason.

* * *

In the end, Lila revealed that she had spared my life because she had already consumed three other victims from a plane crash and wasn't as hungry as she had anticipated. However, she left me stranded on a rooftop from which I couldn't find a way down. I couldn't help but worry if Amara, Ria, and Cake were among her previous victims. Despite feeling hopeless, I held onto the belief that they were still out there.

Lila's strange behavior continued to unsettle me during my confinement on the roof. She frequently asked about my relationship with Lilith, which triggered traumatic memories and made me uncomfortable. Despite my attempts to explain my connection with Lilith, Lila would sneer at me and dismissively label me as a naive human. She seemed fixated on comprehending why Lilith would be intrigued by someone like me.

Things went from bad to worse when Lila started using the threat of eating me as a means of getting satisfactory answers to her questions. Her condescending tone and creepy behavior made me feel sick to my stomach. It became clear that my survival on the island depended not on Lila losing her appetite but on her twisted fascination with Lilith's relationship with me. She incessantly questioned and probed, driving me to the brink of insanity.

As the days wore on, Lila's demeanor grew more and more disturbing. Her gaze would often drift off into the distance, lost in deep contemplation, leaving me to wonder what dark thoughts were consuming her mind. Her behavior took a disconcerting turn when she began to toy with the idea of consuming me as her next meal, relishing in the power dynamic between us. Her twisted game involved watching me squirm and panic as she teasingly reached out with her hand, her fingers curling into sharp claws. It was a chilling display of dominance that left me feeling helpless and vulnerable in her presence.

Trapped on the rooftop with her, I felt like I was living a never-ending nightmare. I longed to escape her unnerving presence and return to a semblance of normalcy. However, I had no choice but to endure her sadistic behavior and hope to make it through each day unharmed.

Although Lila eventually stopped asking about Lilith, her obsession with teasing and tormenting me only intensified. She seemed to delight in the power she held over me, often forcing me into her mouth to endure the stench of her breath and the smell of decay filling my sinuses, or pretending to swallow me whole before stopping at the very last moment. It felt as if she was inflicting pain on me for her entertainment, as though my discomfort was a source of amusement for her.

No matter how much I tried to reason with her, she remained impervious to my pleas, and the fear of her devouring me never left my mind. It was a constant weight on my conscience, a fear that I could never fully shake off. The trauma of my experience with Lila would stay with me for a long time.

* * *

Chapter 7 "Cosmic Despair"

After enduring days of torment, I had lost all hope and given in to my fate. I sat motionless, staring blankly at the ledges of my makeshift concrete open cell prison, resigned to the inevitable. Then, to my surprise, Lila appeared and revealed her twisted form of mercy.

With a cold demeanor and a hint of reluctance, she explained that she spared me only because I was the last link to her beloved sister, Lilith. Despite her yearning for her sister and even acknowledging the reasons why Lilith had developed feelings for me, Lila regarded me as nothing more than an object of fascination and control - a pet.

To my relief, Lila began to provide me with water and sustenance in the form of leaves and fruits, sometimes accompanied by stolen items from victims. I had no other option but to partake in her offerings to survive. However, being around Lila made me even more uneasy. Her pity was just as disturbing as her threats, and I couldn't help but feel like a caged animal.

* * *

For weeks, I had been trapped in a nightmare of isolation and agony, hearing nothing but my own screams. Then, one day, I heard human voices. But their conversation was cut short by blood-curdling screams that made me wish for the familiar silence.

That was when I saw Lilith lift a young woman to her mouth and swallow her whole, leaving me feeling hollow and broken. How could anyone be capable of such monstrous acts? Yet, as the days passed, I found myself growing desensitized to the horror and accepting it as the new reality.

Amid this darkness, Lilith would visit me on the rooftop, sharing stories of her past life and memories with me. Though these moments offered a fleeting glimpse of light, they also highlighted the monstrous nature of my captor. Her visits felt more like a master checking on their pet than a genuine human interaction, and her collection of victims cast a shadow of death and despair over me.

Desperate to hold onto my sanity, I clung to memories of my past life and spoke to myself more frequently. The screams of Lilith's victims echoed in my mind like a never-ending nightmare, tormenting me day and night. Though I thought I was desensitized to it all, the constant trauma proved otherwise.

I was a mere shell of who I used to be, but a small flame of hope kept me from giving up entirely. Maybe someday, I could escape this hell and return to a semblance of normalcy. But deep down, I knew that the odds were slim, and the darkness would never truly leave me.

* * *

One day, something changed. Lila had left to search for more "food" and was gone for a long time. It was then that I finally decided that I couldn't take it anymore. I was tired of being trapped and living like this. I decided to take control of my fate, so I decided to jump from the roof, hoping for a chance at freedom, or at the very least, an end to my suffering. As I walked over to the edge of the roof, I took in all the sights and sounds slowly. I looked down at the street far below me, feeling a mix of fear and excitement. For a moment, I hesitated, wondering if jumping was the right choice. But then I remembered the horrors I had endured - the endless suffering and despair. I knew that I couldn't go on living like that.

My toes hung off the edge of the rooftop as I closed my eyes and took a deep breath, preparing to leap. The wind whipped my hair around my face, and my heart pounded against my chest like a drum. The fear that had been gnawing at me for weeks had finally become too much to bear, and I was ready to end it all.

But then, a sound cut through the silence. It was a megaphone, and I recognized the voice that called out to me. It was Amara, along with Ria and Cake, in an airship hovering above me. I stared up in shock, unable to believe my eyes. How had they found me? And why hadn't Lila noticed the giant airship in the sky?

As the airship lowered a rope ladder down to the rooftop, relief, and joy flooded through me. My heart raced with excitement as I realized I was finally being rescued. I eagerly grabbed onto the ladder's rungs, my fingers trembling with anticipation. I climbed up as fast as I could, longing to be back on solid ground and away from the terror that had consumed me for what felt like an eternity.

But as I climbed, the sound of loud thumping echoed through the air. It was Lila, hot on their tail, her fury palpable even from this distance.

"I finally found you!" Lila yelled at the airship, her voice hoarse and strained. Her eyes locked onto me as I climbed the ladder, and her rage boiled over. "What do you think you're doing?" she yelled at me, her face twisted into a snarl. Tears welled up in her eyes, but they didn't fall. "How dare you, after everything I've done! You insolent, little, pathetic bug!"

Chapter 8 "The Great Escape!"

As the airship began to move, I clung on tightly for dear life while Lila pursued us, demolishing buildings in her path with wild fury. She screamed and wept, tears streaming down her face as we attempted to escape her grasp. "Damn you!" Lila yelled, "Stop running!"

As we flew through a narrow row of buildings, things got very tense. We had to slow the airship down to ensure more control as we squeezed through with Lila close behind. We were only inches away from the walls and approaching a dead end. Seeing the imminent danger and in a lapse of judgment, I decided to cause a distraction and swung from the ladder like a madman, throwing myself through a building's missing window. I yelled at Lila, diverting her attention to me, and then ran through an abandoned office with her smashing everything behind me. Regretting my decision, I eventually reached an office conference room and hid under a table. I could hear constant crashing, and Lila yelling, "Where the hell are you? When I find you, I'm going to make you suffer and beg for death!"

Three gunshots rang out, and the conference room window shattered, revealing a ladder. Without hesitation, I climbed out and looked up to see Amara holding a smoking revolver at the entrance to the airship. Lila noticed and gave chase just as we were approaching a cliff wall, flying through a row of buildings and narrowly dodging one, which sent Lila face-first into the building.

We managed to evade Lila and fly over the cliff wall that enclosed the city, feeling a sense of relief. However, our relief was short-lived as Lila was not about to give up that easily. She ripped off a chunk of the building and hurled it at us, narrowly missing us by inches. Her rage fueled her ascent as she began to climb after us with fierce determination. We soared over the forest, scanning for any sign of Lila behind us, our hearts racing with anticipation. Suddenly, she burst through the dense tree cover, having completed her perilous ascent up the steep cliff wall.

As the airship rose higher, Lila's fury grew more intense. She reached for a nearby large tree branch and hurled it towards us with all her might, narrowly missing the ship's hull. Cake's hands shook as she struggled to maintain control of the vessel.

Cake was working feverishly at the controls, trying to increase the airship's altitude, but it was no use. Lila was gaining on us. Her desperation was palpable, and her eyes burned with fierce determination.

I could feel Amara's gaze on me, urging me to climb faster. I was determined to reach the top, but my arms and legs felt heavy with exhaustion. All I could do was hang on. With each passing moment, Lila drew closer, her rage and frustration filling the air.

Chapter 8 "The Great Escape!"

As Lila closed in on us, the airship began to make evasive maneuvers, juking and dodging in an attempt to outrun her. But Lila was determined to get her revenge, and she wasn't about to give up that easily. Her screams of rage and desperation echoed behind us, punctuated by the sound of trees being smashed apart in her wake.

* * *

Lila disappeared into the trees and suddenly reappeared, her enormous hand reaching out for me as I clung to the ladder of the airship for dear life. The ship shook violently as she struck the ladder with her massive fingers, almost causing me to slip. I could see the terror in Amara's eyes as she rushed to my aid, tying a retractable rope around herself at the airship entrance. Lila was relentless, giving up on using her hands and instead launching herself up from the ground, jaws wide open as she aimed to chomp at me with her mouth. The ladder tore and ripped as she bit into it, and I found myself barely hanging on to the airship.

Suddenly, the ladder gave way, and I gasped as I plummeted toward Lila's gnashing teeth, certain that I was done for. But before I could even scream, Amara sprang into action, throwing herself through the air toward me and catching me in her outstretched arms. Ria, meanwhile, frantically retracted the rope to haul us both back to safety.

* * *

As we soared away on the airship, the wind whipping past our faces, I could hear Lila's furious roar of frustration echoing behind us, making my heart race with adrenaline. For a moment, I was too stunned to even breathe, my mind reeling from the narrowness of our escape.

As Ria pulled us up into the airship with the rope, I couldn't help but glance back at Lila one last time. She stood below us, her face twisted with anguish as she watched us fade into the distance. I could see the tears streaming down her face, her cries of desperation and sorrow for her sister still ringing in my ears.

Despite all the pain and trauma she had inflicted upon me, I was struck with a twinge of guilt and empathy for her desperate situation. But I knew I couldn't let my guard down. The memories of her tormenting me and the fear that she had instilled in me for so long were still fresh in my mind, making it hard to fully trust her.

As we flew further and further away, Lila grew smaller and smaller in the distance, until she was nothing more than a speck on the horizon. But the memory of her anguished cries and tear-streaked face stayed with me, a reminder of the complicated and often conflicting emotions that came with our escape.

* * *

Overwhelmed by the weight of the past weeks, I finally break down in tears. Amara comes to my side, and immediately wraps her arms around me, holding me close to her chest. Her touch is warm and comforting, and I feel the tension in my body slowly dissipate. I bury my face in her shoulder and let the tears flow freely.

Chapter 8 "The Great Escape!"

Between sobs, I manage to tell Amara everything: how Lila captured me, used me as a pet, and attempted to kill me. I describe the endless days and nights I spent locked up on the roof, terrified of being devoured alive. I recount Lila's twisted obsession with her sister, which opened up old wounds and trauma. The screams of the victims still ring in my head, and I was powerless to do anything but listen.

As I speak, Amara listens with a deep sense of empathy and understanding. Her heartbeat against my ear is a soothing rhythm that helps to calm me down. Cake tries to inject some levity into the situation with a joke, but Ria shuts her down with a stern look. They both know how important it is for me to get this all out.

I feel small and vulnerable in Amara's embrace, but I also feel safe and protected. I've always relied on her strength, but now I realize just how much she cares for me. As we fly away from danger, I feel a deep sense of gratitude for her unwavering support.

Nestled in her arms, I let myself cry. It's like a dam has burst inside me, and all the emotions I've been holding in come rushing out. Not just about Lila, but also about Lilith, and everything else that's happened. Amara keeps whispering reassurances in my ear, telling me that I'm safe now and that she's here for me. And I believe her. For the first time in weeks, I feel like maybe everything will be okay.

**

After a while, I start to calm down, and Amara releases me from her embrace. As I wipe away the tears from my eyes, I look up at her and express my gratitude, saying, 'Thank you. I don't know what I would have done without you.' She responds with a warm smile and says, 'You don't have to thank me. That's what friends are for.' Ria and Cake nod in agreement from their positions on the ship.

Curiosity about how they found me piques my interest, so I ask Amara, 'How did you manage to locate me?' To my surprise, she replies, 'I placed a tracker on you.' Taken aback by her response, I inquired as to when she had done it. Amara explains, 'I placed the tracker on your shoulder while I was trying to convince Ria and Cake to help.'

As I feel around my shoulder, I notice a lump and become even more curious and somewhat apprehensive. I probe further and ask her why she had placed the tracker on me. Initially hesitant and flustered, she eventually confesses, 'I track what I want to steal.' This confession leaves me even more puzzled, so I inquire about what she wanted to steal. With confidence and sternness in her tone, she replies, 'Your heart.'

I was at a loss for words and didn't know how to react, so I remained silent, trying to process her statement. Ria chuckles to herself, muttering, 'Same old Amara,' as she digs into her satchel to retrieve an old, broken tracker. A single tear streams down her cheek as she looks down at it.

* * *

We sat in silence for a while, each lost in our thoughts, while the gentle

Chapter 8 "The Great Escape!"

hum of the airship's engine served as soothing background noise. I felt Amara's comforting presence beside me and couldn't help but feel grateful to have her.

As we continued on our journey, I gathered the courage to break the silence and asked Amara, "Hey, can you tell me more about how you guys survived the plane crash and found the airship?"

Amara took a deep breath before beginning her explanation. "After the plane crash, we found ourselves stranded in the middle of a mysterious desert with very little food or water. We had to rely on our survival skills to find shelter and scavenge for resources to stay alive," she explained.

Cake chimed in, saying, "I remember when we found that cactus that had water inside. It was thorny, but it ended up being a lifesaver!"

"Unfortunately, my hand is still hurting from those thorns," they added.

"Fortunately," Amara nodded, "we eventually came across an 'abandoned' airship that a group of pirates had left behind. This stroke of good luck meant we didn't have to risk attacking the heavily armed outpost we had initially planned on stealing from. Initially, we were hesitant about taking the airship, but we knew we had to find a way out of the desert."

Ria enthusiastically chimed in, "Thanks to Amara's exceptional leadership and thieving skills, we were able to successfully steal the abandoned airship from the pirates without much resistance."

Cake interjected, "Although I must admit, a couple of them were not too thrilled about us borrowing their ship. However, with Amara's quick thinking and a well-placed cactus to the frontal lobe by yours truly, we managed to convince them to let us go unharmed."

Amara smirked and shrugged modestly at the compliments. "It was nothing, just a simple distraction, and some smooth talking."

Cake interjected, "Yeah, but it wasn't a complete walk in the park. I had to figure out how to get the airship to fly. It wasn't exactly in the best condition when we found it, but with a little bit of ingenuity, I managed to get it up and running. After many hours of tinkering and analyzing the ship, I discovered that the engine needed a complete overhaul. Luckily, I was able to scavenge parts from other parts of the ship to get it working again. It was touch and go for a while, but eventually, we were able to take off and fly away from that desert wasteland."

Ria jumped in with a playful comment, "She just turned it off and on!" The three chuckled.

Cake retorted to Ria's comment with a playful eye-roll, "Hey, it may have looked like that to you, but it was a lot more complicated than just turning it off and on. But thanks for the vote of confidence!" She grinned, knowing that Ria was just teasing her.

Amara paused for a moment before continuing, "And it wasn't just about getting the airship to fly. Cake also had to navigate through some rough terrain to get us to safety. It was a difficult journey, but we made it out thanks to her." She looked at Cake and smiled warmly. "You're a true asset to the team."

Ria chuckled and said, "Yeah, but don't let it get to your head, Cake. We all played a part in getting us out of there."

As Amara finished her explanation, I felt a mix of emotions - relief that they were able to survive and find a way out of the desert but also guilt that I was the reason they were there in the first place.

"We had to get our friend home, no matter the cost," Amara says, putting a hand on my shoulder. her voice filled with determination "So let's get you home."

Chapter 9 "The Battle In The Sky!"

For several days, our flight over the islands was uneventful. Amara and I passed the time chatting, playing card games, and reading a book on marine biology. Despite the serene views and breathtaking sunsets, I couldn't shake off the nightmares about Lilith that kept haunting me. Adding Lila to the mix only made them worse.

Whenever I woke up sweating and trembling from a particularly vivid nightmare, I would step outside to breathe in the salty air and gaze at the starry sky. There, I would feel Amara's reassuring presence behind me, and I would take comfort in her warmth. However, as I looked up at the twinkling stars, memories of my past life flooded my mind, bringing up painful feelings of inadequacy, frustration, and hopelessness.

I remembered the constant financial struggles, the crushing debt, and the soulless jobs that I had endured for years. I remembered how I had cried out for help, but no one had come to my rescue. And then, I thought about Lilith and how she had appeared out of nowhere, offering

Chapter 9 "The Battle In The Sky!"

me a glimpse of a life that I had never dared to dream of before.

Despite everything that had happened, I couldn't help but feel grateful to Lilith for showing me a different path. She had given me a taste of adventure, passion, and freedom that had been missing from my life for so long. And even though she had caused me so much pain, I couldn't bring myself to hate her completely. As I looked up at the stars, I realized that my journey with Lilith was not over yet and that I had to find a way to make peace with my past if I ever wanted to move forward.

* * *

On one particularly quiet day, the airship shook violently as the sounds of cannons and gunfire filled the cabin. Panic-stricken shouts from my friends filled the air as they scrambled to fight off the attackers.

"We're surrounded!" Ria's voice cut through the chaos. "All hands on deck!"

As Amara stormed into my room, her eyes burned with fierce determination. She locked eyes with me and wasted no time in making her intentions clear. "We need you to help us fight," her voice rang with a sense of urgency.

Despite my fear and uncertainty, I listened to her impassioned speech. She reminded me of the skills I honed while surviving on the island, urging me to draw upon that experience now. Her words bolstered me, and I felt a flicker of hope ignite within me.

Without hesitation, I made my way to the back of the ship where the mounted machine guns awaited. Each step quickened my heart rate and nerves, but I steeled myself for the battle ahead.

Reaching the gun, I took a deep breath and steadied my hands. The weight of the weapon felt reassuring in my grip. As I peered out of the window, my eyes widened in terror at the sight of the attacking pirate airships surrounding us. My hands trembled with fear as I steadied my aim, trying to focus on the approaching targets.

With a deafening roar and a nearly blinding flash of fire, my shot hit one of the pirate ships' engines, causing it to explode in a fiery blast. The explosion sent debris raining down on the other pirate ships, causing chaos and confusion among their ranks.

I let out an exuberant whoop as the smell of burning fuel and smoke filled the air. The pirates frantically attempted to maneuver their ships out of harm's way, but we kept up the attack.

As the battle raged on, we fought fiercely, united in our goal to protect ourselves and each other. The wind whipped through our hair, and the clash of metal and the sound of gunfire echoed around us.

With each successful hit, my confidence grew, and my fear dissipated. The adrenaline rush surged through my veins as we continued to defend our ship, determined not to let the pirates get the upper hand.

Chapter 9 "The Battle In The Sky!"

* * *

The sounds of gunfire filled the air as Cake's panicked voice crackled through the commotion. "I'm trying to evade them, but they're gaining on us! We need more power to the engines!"

Ria sprang into action, her focus unbroken as she rushed to the engine room. Despite the chaos around her, her hands moved quickly, rerouting power to the engines. "Hang on tight, Cake! I'm doing everything I can!"

Amara's commanding voice boomed through the intercom, and my heart raced with adrenaline. She called for my help, and I raced to her side of the ship. The pirates were closing in, slimy and smirking, armed to the teeth. I watched as Amara's revolver gleamed in the sunlight, firing round after round. But there were too many pirates, and Amara was beginning to tire.

I grabbed the machine gun and instinctively aimed it toward the pirates, firing accurately and hitting the bridge, causing the pirates to fall. Amara smiled and beckoned me to follow her. We rushed to the side of the ship, taking positions behind a machine gun. She instructed me to man the gun while she stood behind me, covering our backs. Despite the deafening sounds of gunfire and explosions from the relentless pirate attack, I could feel the heat of the gun in my hand as I mowed down any pirate who dared to approach us. Amara remained beside me, her eyes sharp and focused as she took down pirate after pirate from behind.

Suddenly, a loud boom echoes through the air as Cake accidentally finds the cannon controls and fires a shot. We all freeze for a moment, stunned by the power of the cannons, which blow an enemy airship out of the sky. Ria, who had been frantically patching up the ship, bursts onto the scene and rips a machine gun off a mount before joining the fight with fierce determination. She aims at the engines of the different pirate airships, causing them to plummet into the ocean below.

Together, the four of us fight off the pirates with all our might. The battle is brutal, and by the time it's over, we are all covered in sweat and grime. Despite the damage sustained, we somehow manage to emerge victorious, with the ship still intact and flying. As the battle finally draws to a close, we catch our breath and take stock of our situation.

* * *

Amara turns to me, her eyes sparkling with admiration. "You were incredible out there. I couldn't have done it without you," she says, her voice filled with gratitude.

I smile at her, feeling a sense of satisfaction that we had successfully defended ourselves against the sky pirates. As we chat about our battle strategy, Cake interrupts us by waving a small tracking device in front of our faces.

"Look what I found!" she exclaims, her excitement contagious. Amara and I exchanged a curious glance, wondering what Cake had in mind.

Taking the device from Cake, Ria examines it closely, her brow furrowed in concentration. Amara, with a mischievous grin on her face, snatches the device from Ria's hand and begins tinkering with it.

"You know, we could have a little fun with this," she says, winking at us. We all look at her expectantly as she works her magic on the device.

After a few hours, Amara announces that she's hacked into the pirate's tracking signal and can now manipulate it to show a false location. We all stare at her in awe as she explains her plan. She suggests placing the fake tracking signal on the island where Lila resides, hoping the pirates will chase after it while we make our escape.

Without hesitation, we all agree to the plan, eager to outsmart the pirates who had just attacked us . Amara sets the device to display a fake signal on the island, and we settle in to wait for the pirates to take the bait.

* * *

Days passed, and we continued our journey, each mile taking us further away from the pirates who had pursued us. Relief coursed through me as we flew, knowing our plan had worked and that we had outsmarted them. But I couldn't help feeling a twinge of guilt, knowing what Lila was likely capable of doing to the pirates who had tracked us. Yet, I pushed the thought aside; I hated pirates, and they had gotten what they deserved.

As we flew for several more days, the airship began to show the wear and tear of the pirate attack. Ria and Cake assessed the situation and determined that we needed to make an emergency landing. The landing was jarring, and we stumbled out of the cabin, taking in the damage with a mix of shock and dismay. The hull was visibly dented, and our gear was scattered about.

Despite the chaos and setback we had faced, there was a glimmer of hope that pierced through the darkness. Cake pulled out a map and traced her finger across its surface, stopping at a location just a stone's throw away from my home. "We're so close," she said, "we can take a plane from here if we have to."

A sense of relief and excitement surged within me at the thought of being back home after such a long time. But amidst the joy, a nagging feeling of unease crept up on me. It felt like an invisible hand was squeezing the pit of my stomach, warning me of new, unseen dangers lurking around the corner.

As I tried to shake off the feeling, I couldn't help but wonder what lay ahead. The journey had already been filled with so much peril and uncertainty, and the thought of facing more challenges was daunting.

Chapter 9 "The Battle In The Sky!"

Chapter 10 "The Consequences of Love"

As we set up camp for the night, my mind wanders to Lilith, and I can't help but think about what I'll do when we finally reach my home. Will I turn her in, or will I forgive her and try to get her help? Despite all the terrible things Lilith has done and the nightmares that haunt me, my feelings toward her are in a constant state of conflict. It's hard to shake the belief that she was a victim of circumstance. Perhaps, with the right kind of help, she could be saved from the path she's chosen. But then again, is it deep-seated love that's keeping me from letting go of her, as any reasonable person would?

The truth is, Lilith's actions have caused immense pain and suffering to those around her. Her hunger has led her down a path of darkness, where she's become blind to the consequences of her actions. It's difficult to see her as a victim when the harm she's caused is so evident. The weight of the decision hangs heavily on my mind, and I know that I'll have to make a choice soon. I turn to face my companions and ask for their advice. I can see the uncertainty etched on their faces as they contemplate my question. After a moment of contemplation, Amara

Chapter 10 "The Consequences of Love"

clears her throat and her voice takes on a serious tone.

"Lilith may have been your lover, but she also took the lives of innocent people," she says, her gaze unwavering. "You must decide what is right, but you must also consider the consequences of your actions."

Ria solemnly nods her agreement, adding her perspective to the conversation. "Sometimes, doing what is right is the hardest choice we must make," she says. "But we must always remember that our actions have consequences."

Cake breaks the tension in the air with a comment that leaves us all taken aback. "Remember the time I accidentally killed a man with a syrup bottle for harassing ya, Ria?" she says. "That had consequences."

Ria rolls her eyes at the memory. "Please don't remind me," she says. "You were lucky to get off with a warning, considering how much of a creep and monster he was."

Amara looks at Cake with a puzzled expression. "Wait, you killed a man with a syrup bottle?" she asks, genuinely curious about the strange turn of events.

"Don't get her started!" Ria cuts in, her tone slightly annoyed. "We need to stay on track."

Ria then turns to me, speaking with firm yet compassionate words. "Jon, I understand that Lilith was your soulmate, but what she did was unforgivable," she says. "She took innocent lives, and there are consequences to that. You have to think about what's right, not just for yourself, but for the people she hurt."

Cake stays silent, sensing the gravity of the conversation. She takes a deep breath and speaks slowly as if carefully selecting her words. "Sometimes, doing the right thing is not the easiest or most obvious choice," she says. "It requires us to examine our values and ourselves to make a decision. We must weigh the consequences of our actions and consider the possible impact they will have on others. It's not about what we want but what is genuinely right."

After Cake's profound but vague answer, we sat in silence for a few moments, each of us reflecting on our own beliefs and values, as it seemed to awaken something deep within us.

* * *

Later that night, I had a dream about Lilith. In the dream, we ran through fields of brightly colored flowers, while the sweet fragrance of blooming petals filled the air around us. We danced together under the starry night sky, and our laughter echoed across the fields. Suddenly, we were lifted off the ground and soared through the clouds, while the wind whipped through our hair.

As we flew higher and higher, the world below faded away until there was nothing but the vast expanse of the starry sky above us. Despite the dizzying heights and speed, I felt completely safe with Lilith by my side.

The dream felt like pure magic, and I couldn't help but feel an overwhelming sense of joy and contentment. It was as if nothing else in the world mattered except for the moment we were sharing together.

Chapter 10 "The Consequences of Love"

We landed on a hilltop overlooking a breathtaking view, and Lilith turned to me, taking my hand. "This is our world," she said, looking deep into my eyes. "A world where anything is possible."

I smiled back at her, feeling an intense connection that I couldn't quite explain. In this dream, I felt like I was truly living, experiencing everything the world had to offer. And for once, I felt like everything was going to be okay. But then my dream quickly turned into a nightmare: Lilith evaporated, and a giant pale hand reached out to crush me. With all my strength, I managed to escape the hand's grasp and jumped off a white sharp cliff, landing on the scalp of a person with black hair and two fox ears, each pierced with two gold rings. My heart raced with fear as a hand reached to pick me up, and I was very anxious about the owner of the hand. To my relief, it was Amara who looked at me to check if I was okay before placing me in her red jacket pocket. She scanned the area to assess my pursuers. Her hand swiftly moved to her holster, and she pulled out her revolver, ready to fight off whatever was coming our way.

She quickly dispensed 6 rounds from her revolver into the giant pale hand pursuing me, and it dissipated into a mist. Suddenly, a dense mist appeared before us, slowly morphing into a towering Lilith. Amara wasted no time in swiftly reloading her revolver, her fingers moving with practiced precision. However, before she could even take aim, Lilith reached out for the pocket I was in.

Amara's reflexes kicked in as she reacted with lightning speed, throwing a powerful punch toward Lilith. The blow connected with a sickening thud, and Lilith's body disintegrated into a dissipating mist as it crashed onto the ground. More hands and Liliths appeared, looking more hellish than the last. Despite the overwhelming odds, Amara continued to fight, taking on one enemy after another with her quick reflexes and expert marksmanship.

As I watched Amara fight, I felt a mix of fear and admiration. She was a true warrior, and I was grateful to have her on my side. With her help, we managed to defeat many of the creatures.

* * *

I watch in awe as Amara takes down the last of the demonic hands. Her movements are graceful and precise as if she has been fighting her entire life. Suddenly, an enormous figure of Lilith looms over us, and I feel dread wash over me. This is the person who has caused me so much pain and heartache, yet a part of me still longs for her.

The battle between Amara and Lilith is fierce, with both sides giving their all. Lilith is a formidable opponent, with strength and power beyond anything I have ever seen, but Amara is a force to be reckoned with and refuses to back down.

As Lilith hurls attacks at us, Amara fires her gun, running, ducking, and dodging. The sound of gunfire fills the air, and my heart races with each shot. It's intense, almost too much to bear, but I can't look away.

Finally, with a powerful shot, Amara strikes Lilith down. For a moment, there's silence, and I'm not sure if Lilith is dead or just stunned. But then, she begins to weep, saying "I'm sorry" over and over again. Despite all the trauma and pain she's caused, seeing her reduced to tears is a sobering sight.

Chapter 10 "The Consequences of Love"

As we begin to walk away from Lilith, the dream fades away. I wake up in the middle of the night, feeling a deep sense of realization wash over me. The dream was a sign, a message from my subconscious telling me to let go of the past and embrace the present. As I lay there, I start to feel a newfound appreciation for Amara and all she has done for me. She's always been there for me, through thick and thin, and her unwavering support and love have been a constant in my life ever since she entered it.

At that moment, I couldn't help but feel disgusted with myself for even considering the idea of giving Lilith another chance. The thought of attempting to rehabilitate someone who has committed such heinous crimes and caused so much trauma was repulsive to me. It's now clear to me that I need to focus on the people who are truly important in my life, such as Amara, and leave the past where it belongs. However, I know that it will be easier said than done, but I'll give it a damn good try.

With a newfound sense of clarity and purpose, I drift back to sleep, feeling grateful for the dream that helped me see the truth.

Suddenly, I am jolted awake by the distant rumbling of tanks and the sound of guns being drawn. My heart races as I sit up and scan our surroundings, only to find that my companions, Amara, and the others, are already awake and alert. In the distance, I can see airships looming, flickering with a dim light that casts an eerie glow on our campsite.

"What's going on?" I whisper, my voice barely audible.

Amara's eyes dart back and forth, scanning the area for any sign of danger. "I'm not sure," she replies, "but we need to be prepared for anything."

Suddenly, a group of soldiers appears from the trees, their weapons at the ready. They demand that we surrender, and before we can even react, we are on our knees, handcuffed, and taken away in a military vehicle. My mind races with questions, but the soldiers remain tight-lipped as they take us to a compound and throw us into a nearby jail cell.

"I can't believe this is happening," I thought to myself as my mind was flooded with terrifying possibilities. Straining to hear any muffled sounds of soldiers or guards outside, I hoped for some clue as to what was going on. All I could do was wait and pray that we would be released soon, realizing that our fate rested in the hands of others.

* * *

In the jail later, I could hear Ria and Cake talking to each other in the cell next to us. I tried to eavesdrop on their conversation to see if they had any information about what was going on, but they were speaking in hushed tones, and I couldn't make out much.

After a while, I decided to try and strike up a conversation with them. "Hey, guys, do you have any idea what's going on here?" I asked, trying to keep my tone casual.

Ria turned towards me, her expression guarded. "We don't know much," she said. "We were just camping nearby when those soldiers showed up and took us in."

Chapter 10 "The Consequences of Love"

Cake nodded in agreement. "Yeah, we didn't do anything wrong. We're just innocent bystanders."

I nodded, but I couldn't help feeling like there was more to the story. I decided to press them a little more. "Do you have any idea who these soldiers are? Why are they here?"

Ria and Cake exchanged a look before Ria spoke up. "We heard some of the soldiers talking earlier. They're part of a rebellion group that's trying to overthrow the government."

My eyes widened in surprise. "A rebellion? What do they want?"

"I don't know," Cake said with a shrug. "But it doesn't sound good."

A prisoner with a thick accent caught our attention by knocking on his cell across from us. "Excuse me," he said, "I couldn't help but overhear your conversation. I believe I can provide some insight into the rebellion." Intrigued, we welcomed him to the conversation, and he introduced himself as Aldrich, a former leader of the rebellion who had been arrested for his dissenting views.

Aldrich began to describe the horrors of living under a tyrannical government controlled by a few corporations. "They charged for everything and anything, even the most basic necessities for survival. They poisoned the water supply and crops, allowing many to die of famine and homelessness. Those who survived and made just enough to get by were poisoned with propaganda that never explained the true extent of their oppression. It was a hellscape for the poor, while the wealthy at the top lived in luxury, profiting from their misery."

While Aldrich believed in the fight for freedom, he disagreed with the way the rebellion was being conducted. "They managed to take this region, but they are disorganized, and there's a lot of infighting on what to do. They arrest any and all people, like you foreigners, and force them to join the front lines." He explained that we couldn't escape now, but on the front lines, we might have a chance.

After careful consideration of the high stakes, Ria and Cake concluded that I did not possess the necessary combat experience to survive in a war zone's dangerous and unpredictable environment. Despite gaining experience from the battle on the airship, they remained unconvinced that it was sufficient to prepare me for what lay ahead. Instead, they turned their attention to Amara, who, despite her skills and combat experience, lacked war zone experience and did not want to leave me alone in a mysterious prison. They knew that I needed someone I could trust and rely on to help me navigate the unfamiliar and potentially dangerous situation. As they looked at Amara, she met Ria's gaze with a determined expression, and Ria nodded back at her with a small smile.

So, the two of them put their heads together and devised a daring plan. They would offer themselves up to the rebellion, pretending to join their cause in exchange for access to weapons and information. It was a risky move, but they were willing to take the chance. Once they had gathered enough intel, they would use the weapons to stage a prison break and escape the rebellion's grasp.

"It's a bold plan," Ria admitted, "but it's our best shot at getting out of here alive."

Cake nodded in agreement. "We'll need to be careful not to blow our cover," she said. "We don't want to end up on the wrong side of the rebellion."

I looked at them both with concern. "What if things go wrong?"

Ria gave me a reassuring smile. "We'll stick together and get through it. That's all we can do."

Aldrich tells us that the guards will come to take him away soon, but before they do, he offers to help us. "I'll let them know that Ria and Cake are interested in joining the rebellion," he says. "It will expedite the process, and they won't have to go through the usual two-week hold and re-education time."

They nod their heads in agreement, grateful for his help.

* * *

As the guards came to take Aldrich away, he told them that Ria and Cake were interested in joining the rebellion. Soon after, the guards collected Ria and Cake from their cells. As they walked by, Ria gave a subtle wink to Amara, who, in turn, revealed a small tracker hidden in her headband. With a quick motion, Amara removed the tracker from under her yellow headband and passed the receiver to Ria, all while keeping a watchful eye on their surroundings. We all understood that this small device could be our only chance of escape from this treacherous place. As Ria and Cake disappeared into a nearby corridor, we waved goodbye, knowing that they were our only hope of getting out of here.

"Amara, do you think they will make it back in time?" I asked, my voice barely above a whisper.

"Yes, there's no way they won't," she replied confidently, her eyes locked onto mine. I wanted to believe her, but a part of me couldn't shake the feeling that we were doomed.

***

A few days had passed since our captivity, and I couldn't help but wonder why fate had put me in this situation yet again. However, this time I had Amara with me, and our captors surprised us with decent meals and a table to dine on, making our imprisonment a bit more bearable.

One guard, in particular, stood out from the others. Sylvia, with her brown hair, green eyes, and freckles, wore a red beret atop her camo uniform. She visited our cell frequently, engaging us in conversations about her life and our experiences, bringing a glimmer of hope to our bleak surroundings.

During her visits, Sylvia would often bring extra food. We soon noticed her special attention to Amara as she would flirt with her and find excuses to linger in our cell, which seemed to please Amara.

Sylvia also gave us literature and manifestos about their cause, educating us on their fight against the state of Cormica and their takeover of the region they called Arman. The materials sparked discussions between Amara and me, and we found ourselves intrigued by their cause.

Although we were still prisoners, Sylvia's kindness and attention gave us a brief respite from the harsh reality of our captivity. Her actions, however small, reminded us that not all of our captors were heartless and cruel.

* * *

Amara and I read and discussed literature on a daily basis with Sylvia. We found ourselves increasingly convinced by the author's arguments that healthcare is a fundamental human right that should not be tied to employment or profit. Although I was fortunate enough to have access to universal healthcare back home, I was aware of its limitations - it did not cover dental, for example, and it was not as comprehensive as what the literature suggested was possible.

Our conversations often centered on how healthcare could be improved, both in our home countries and around the world. We talked about the need for greater investment in preventive care, as well as the importance of addressing the social determinants of health, such as poverty and inequality. We also discussed the role of pharmaceutical companies and their influence on healthcare policies and debated the merits of different healthcare models, from single-payer systems to hybrid public-private approaches.

Another passage stood out to me and caused me to reevaluate everything. It discussed how large companies have the power to directly influence laws with little scrutiny, resulting in a fundamentally negative impact on our lives. When I read this, I couldn't help but reflect on my situation back home and wonder how close we were to experiencing a similar hellscape, where our lives were controlled by corporate interests, and the government was powerless to intervene.

Although I still wished we were not being held captive and planned on being sent to war, I came to understand why our captors were fighting. It seemed that nothing else was working, and their living conditions had only deteriorated as the corporations that controlled the country grew more powerful, effectively making the government their puppet. The people had no choice but to band together and form their institutions to meet their needs and stand up against the oppressive corporate regime.

The constant defense of their stronghold, which seemed to get attacked every day, was a testament to their struggle. We heard distant gunfire in the night, and as we lay in our cell, we hoped that Cake and Ria would show up soon. Time was running out as the days went by, and we only had a week left before we were both shipped out to war. Amara held out hope that they would show, but I could not feel it myself. However, I trusted her intuition.

Chapter 11 "Make Love Not War"

As the deadline for our deployment drew near, the daily routine of our prison transformed into a grueling regimen of combat training and briefings. The clanging of weapons and shouting of commands echoed through the hallways, a constant reminder of the impending battle we were being prepared for.

The training was exhausting, and every day brought new bruises and sore muscles. However, the physical pain paled in comparison to the mental toll it was taking on me. The reality of being sent off to war, to fight and possibly die in a foreign land, weighed heavily on my mind. I couldn't shake the feeling of dread and despair that seemed to grow with each passing day.

Unlike me, Amara remained optimistic, even as the deadline drew near. She had faith that Cake and Ria would come to our rescue, and she refused to let the guards' harsh treatment break her spirit.

However, for me, the looming threat of being forced to fight in a war in which we had no stake was suffocating. The guards, including Sylvia, were as kind as they could be under the circumstances, but their forced neutrality only served to highlight the injustice of our situation. The only thing that kept me going was the hope that somehow, against all odds, we would make it out alive.

* * *

One day, on the eve of our deployment to the battlefield, we sat in our cell, listening to distant gunfire. The sound was almost comforting, a familiar background noise to our captivity. Suddenly, there was a deafening explosion that shook the walls of our cell. Dust and debris rained down on us as we huddled together in fear.

We heard footsteps in the hallway, and at first, we thought it was the guards coming to check on us. However, a dying guard stumbled into view instead. It was Sylvia, the kind guard who had visited us and brought us extra food. Her once vibrant green eyes were now dull, and her skin was pale and clammy.

Sylvia unlocked our cell and urged us to run, her voice strained and urgent. We could hear the sound of screams and gunfire getting closer. Sylvia told us that the Cormica forces had arrived and were killing indiscriminately. In her final act of kindness, Sylvia handed over the revolver that had been confiscated from Amara. In return, Amara gave Sylvia a gentle peck on the cheek, a silent gesture of gratitude and farewell.

Chapter 11 "Make Love Not War"

With a serene smile on her face, Sylvia slipped away, leaving Amara with a heavy heart and a sense of loss.

* * *

As we escaped from our cell, Amara led the way with her eyes fixed on the path ahead and her revolver tightly gripped in her hand. The sound of gunfire grew louder with each step, and we knew that our time was running out. I followed closely behind her, my heart pounding in my chest as we darted through the dark passageways, avoiding the traps set by the guards.

Suddenly, we turned a corner and found ourselves face-to-face with several armed soldiers, their weapons aimed squarely at us. Amara reacted quickly, raised her revolver, and fired a single shot that took down four soldiers in quick succession. She looked at her weapon in amazement, surprised by her accuracy.

Meanwhile, I grabbed a nearby pipe and charged at the remaining soldier, catching him off-guard with a swift blow that knocked him to the ground. We breathed a sigh of relief as we realized we had overcome this obstacle, but we knew that there were more challenges to come.

As we made our way through the compound, the chaos around us grew more intense. Explosions rocked the walls, and gunfire echoed through the halls as we fought our way toward freedom. Amara's combat skills were nothing short of impressive as she took out enemy after enemy with precision and skill, her revolver blazing like a beacon of hope in the darkness.

The rebels were putting up a valiant fight, but it was clear they were being overwhelmed by the sheer number of attackers. We could see the desperation in their eyes as they fought to protect their home and cause. As we ran, I couldn't help but feel a sense of guilt that we were escaping while they stayed to fight.

There was no time for second-guessing; we had to keep moving if we wanted to make it out alive. As we turned the corner, we found ourselves face-to-face with a group of soldiers who were unloading their weapons into a rebel on the ground while holding another at gunpoint, forcing them to watch.

Without hesitation, Amara fired her weapon with deadly accuracy, freeing the hostage who then thanked her and offered her a machine gun. We dashed away, running down a narrow corridor with bullets peppering the walls and narrowly missing us. As we approached the door at the end of the hallway, Amara riddled it with machine gun bullets, sending a soldier tumbling out.

Amara tossed down the now empty machine gun, and we rushed through the door. We had no idea what lay ahead, but we knew that we had to keep moving if we wanted to survive.

In the new corridor, the gunfire intensified as a fierce fight broke out between the rebels and the Cormica soldiers up ahead. Amara instructed me to stay back while she went to aid the rebels in pushing back the soldiers. Reloading her revolver, she darted ahead into the fray. I nodded in agreement, watching her disappear into the chaos before turning my attention to the surrounding area.

I couldn't help but notice how much Amara was giving her all. I had

Chapter 11 "Make Love Not War"

seen her fight on the airship, displaying impressive combat abilities, but today she was going well beyond her skills. She was determined beyond reason to get us out.

Lost in thought, I was suddenly ambushed by a soldier who had been hiding in a nearby cell. We struggled, with him attempting to shoot me with his gun. In a moment of panic, he accidentally discharged the weapon, causing the bullet to ricochet off the wall and strike one of his comrades who was entering through the corridor's entrance. His comrade fell to the ground, wounded.

Furious, the soldier tackled me, and we both crashed to the ground. I struggled to catch my breath as I lay on the ground, feeling the impact of the soldier's tackle. But before I could even gather myself, I saw Amara charging toward us. Her eyes were wild with fury, and she launched herself at the soldier, punching him with all her might.

The soldier staggered back, clearly caught off guard by Amara's ferocity. But he quickly recovered and grabbed hold of her, trying to subdue her. Amara fought back with everything she had, grappling with the soldier as they stumbled toward a group of enemy soldiers.

I tried to crawl away, fearing the worst, when suddenly I saw Amara pull the pin on the soldier's grenade. I froze, watching in horror as the soldier panicked and tried to get away from the grenade. Amara was one step ahead, drop-kicking him toward the group of soldiers and landing on her knees.

The explosion was deafening, and I felt the heat wash over me as the soldiers were engulfed in flames. Amara rushed over to me, helping me to my feet. I could see the pain and exhaustion in her eyes, but she didn't stop moving. She grabbed my arm and dragged me towards the exit, yelling for the rebels to follow us.

We burst out of the compound and into a war zone. Smoke and dust filled the air, and I could see tanks and helicopters circling overhead. But Amara didn't hesitate, pulling me towards a nearby building and urging the rebels to follow.

Inside, we found a group of rebel fighters who had set up a makeshift command center. They were monitoring the battle on a bank of screens, coordinating their forces, and trying to gain ground against the enemy.

Amara quickly took charge, assessed the situation, and offered her help. She handed her revolver to one of the fighters and began barking orders, telling them where to focus their fire and how to outmaneuver the enemy.

For the next few hours, we fight alongside the rebels, taking cover behind walls and firing back at the enemy soldiers. It's intense, exhausting work, but Amara never falters. She's like a force of nature, pushing us forward and driving us toward victory.

As the sun began to set, the sound of distant sirens signaled the enemy's retreat, and we knew we had won the battle. Amara collapsed to the ground, panting and covered in sweat, but a smile spread across her face. I walked over to her and asked what had come over her today, telling her how incredible she was. I questioned why Ria and Cake said that she had no experience in war zones.

"I don't," she replied, "and to be honest, I'm way out of my element," I asked her how she was able to perform and lead so well if she didn't, and she responded with a simple answer. "You," she said, gesturing for me to sit next to her as we watched the sunset.

Amara took a deep breath and began to confess something that weighed heavily on her heart. "I spent years in isolation before I met you," she started, her voice low and hesitant. "I let go of someone I loved because work took precedence, and I attempted to fill the void with material things. But no amount of wealth could fill the emptiness inside me. I took on dangerous jobs, hoping to find a purpose, but I remained lost. Eventually, I accepted a job that went against my values, and it led to my capture and enslavement. My tracker wasn't functioning, and I was alone, so I gave up. I thought my fate was sealed until you came into my life."

As she spoke, I listened intently, my heart breaking for her. Amara had always been my protector, my friend, and my confidante. She risked everything to keep me safe. "When they threw you into my quarters," she continued, "I felt something stir inside me. I found a purpose in you. Since then, I have been trying to steal something far more precious than any treasure I have ever taken - your heart."

Amara looked at me with a mix of hope and fear in her eyes, and said, "You don't have to be afraid anymore. Let me love you." The question caught me off guard, and my heart skipped a beat. Do I love her?

Her words touched me deeply, and I realized that I had been in love with her all along and I'd been using Lilith as an excuse because I'm afraid to love again. She was the missing piece in my life, and without her, I would be incomplete. I looked into her eyes, took her hand, and whispered, "I love you."

Tears pooled in Amara's eyes, and she threw herself, locking me in her arms as the sun set behind us. At that moment, I knew that no matter what lay ahead, as long as we had each other, we could conquer anything.

As the night sky envelops us, Amara and I take a moment to appreciate the beauty of the stars above while sitting together in the forest. The rustling of leaves and the occasional chirp of a cricket fills the air. Suddenly, we hear two voices calling out to us. It's Ria and Cake, and they are surprised to see us outside the compound. Cake jokes, "Oh no, our amazing fantastical plan is ruined. Go back in so we can try it."

Amara and I burst into laughter until a sudden sound interrupts us: the click of a gun. Cake's voice grows stern and She says, "I'm serious." Ria flicks Cake's ear with a serious disapproving expression, and Cake apologizes for taking the joke too far.

**

After catching up on what had happened, Ria winked at Amara and asked if she had done a certain thing. Amara smiled and nodded in response, and Ria laughed before getting down to business. She told us that they had found a contact on the battlefield who had a way out of the country, but we would have to travel through Cormica territory to get there.

As we made our way towards the stolen jeep, Cake started complaining about the food they had while on the front lines. She grumbled about how gross it was, while Ria rolled her eyes and started the engine. We drove off into the mountains, the cool breeze blowing through our hair as we left the past behind.

Amara and I shared a chuckle at Cake's complaining, grateful for the momentary break from the intensity of the situation. As we rode deeper into the mountains, Ria filled us in on their plan to cross into Cormica territory undetected.

She explained that they had secured fake identification papers, but we would still need to be careful and avoid any checkpoints. Cake added that we would also need to be on the lookout for any bounty hunters or other dangerous individuals who might be searching for us.

Chapter 12 "From Armen With Love"

As we drive through the winding mountain roads, Amara and I huddle close together, taking comfort in each other's presence. The night is quiet except for the hum of the jeep's engine and the occasional hooting of an owl.

Cake breaks the silence and starts to rant about the food again. Her complaints become more and more absurd with each passing moment, describing a sandwich so dry it turned to dust in her mouth and a soup that tasted like someone had boiled old socks in it. Amara and I try to keep straight faces, but it becomes harder as Cake's complaints become more ridiculous. At one point, she even claims to have found a hair in her water but realizes upon closer inspection that it was just a thread from her shirt.

We burst out laughing, and even Cake can't help but chuckle at her own ridiculousness. As we drive deeper into the mountains, the four of us chat and joke, the tension from the previous hours fading away. Finally, we arrive at our destination - a small town nestled in the mountains.

Chapter 12 "From Armen With Love"

Ria leads us to a small inn where we settle in for the night, grateful for a warm bed and a roof over our heads. As we drift off to sleep, I can't help but feel grateful for the friends I've made and the adventures we've shared.

***

The next morning, we gathered around a table in a small diner near the border, where Ria and Cake laid out the plan for us. They carefully went over every detail to ensure our safety, and we listened attentively, nodding in understanding as Ria explained how we would navigate through the checkpoints.

As we ate our breakfast, I couldn't help but smile as I watched Amara devour her pancakes with delight. I never would have guessed that she had a sweet tooth, but there she was, happily smearing butter and syrup all over her stack of fluffy pancakes.

Cake, on the other hand, was on a mission to eat as many waffles as humanly possible. Plate after plate of golden-brown waffles was placed in front of her, and she attacked them with a fervor that was both impressive and slightly terrifying.

Ria looked on in a mixture of awe and horror, amazed at the sheer amount of food that Cake was able to consume. "I don't know whether to be impressed or disgusted," she remarked, shaking her head in disbelief.

Despite the distraction of our breakfast, we all knew that we had a dangerous mission ahead of us. However, at that moment, surrounded by the warm glow of the diner and the comforting smell of freshly cooked pancakes and waffles, it was easy to forget the danger and just enjoy each other's company.

* * *

After breakfast, we mounted the jeep and headed toward the checkpoints. Riding through the hills, we had to be careful to avoid detection by the blockade on the narrow bridge by going under it. The jeep jolted and rocked as we maneuvered through the bumpy terrain, but we held on tight.

The next checkpoint required us to jump the jeep over a cliff. Ria pushed the jeep to its limits, revving the engine as we all held onto our seats. The wheels spun and dug into the dirt before propelling us forward, and we soared through the air, barely clearing the cliff's edge. The wind whipped through our hair as we let out a collective breath of relief.

The last checkpoint was relatively easy. We just had to drive around a hill to bypass it. However, the final checkpoint was daunting. There were no other pathways. It was a drawbridge over a deep chasm, and the only way through was by presenting our IDs. We all felt a sense of nervous anticipation as we approached.

As we approached the drawbridge checkpoint, our nerves were on edge. Ria and Cake handed over the IDs to the guards, and we held our breath, hoping they would work. The guards inspected the IDs for what felt like an eternity, scrutinizing every detail, and our hearts sank as they looked at us suspiciously.

Chapter 12 "From Armen With Love"

Just as we thought we were going to get caught, the guards handed back the IDs, and we let out a collective sigh of relief. Ria expertly maneuvered the jeep across the drawbridge, and we made it to the other side undetected.

As we drove away from the checkpoint, the tension in the jeep slowly dissipated, and we all breathed a sigh of relief. We were finally out of enemy territory and on our way to our destination. Amara turned to me and smiled, and I knew that we had all made it through together.

The rest of the journey was relatively uneventful, with Ria and Cake taking turns driving while the rest of us rested. Finally, we arrived at our destination: a small town on the edge of the border, just as the sun was setting. Ria and Cake led us to a safe house where we would be staying for the night, and we settled in for some much-needed rest.

As I lay there, I felt Amara climb in beside me and snuggle up. It was a simple act of comfort, but it meant the world to me at that moment. I woke up to the sound of sizzling bacon and the smell of fresh coffee. Amara was still sleeping soundly beside me, and I gently kissed her forehead before getting out of bed.

In the kitchen, Ria and Cake had already prepared a simple but delicious breakfast of eggs, bacon, and toast. We all sat around the small table and discussed our plans for the day.

Ria and Cake had arranged for us to meet a contact who could help me find a way back home to New Colombia. We were all excited and nervous at the same time, not knowing what to expect.

As we arrived at the meeting point, we saw a man waiting for us. He introduced himself as our contact, and we followed him to a nearby alleyway. However, as soon as we entered, the man revealed himself to be a Cormica soldier in disguise.

Before we could react, the soldier had locked us all in the back of a truck and started driving, causing us to thrash about in the back. We were trapped, and as the truck continued to drive, our anxiety grew about where they were taking us. After a while, we started banging on the walls and yelling, but to no avail. Suddenly, we heard gunfire and explosions outside. The truck had been ambushed by rebels!

The soldiers driving the truck were taken by surprise, and we could hear them fighting back against the rebels outside. Amidst the chaos, the back door of the truck was opened, and we were quickly ushered out by the rebels. They explained that they had followed us from the compound and were there to thank Amara for inspiring them with her leadership skills and bravery. They wanted her to be their leader and offered her a position as a general in their army. However, Amara rejected their offer, explaining that she had to see my journey home through and start a new life with me. She did offer some advice on how to run their operation more efficiently, and they listened intently, thanking her before disappearing into the shadows.

Now alone, we all tried to figure out what to do next. The truck was empty, and we had no idea where we were or what direction to go. But we knew we had to keep moving, so we started walking, hoping to find some help or a way out of the unknown location we found ourselves in.

As we cautiously made our way down the road, we spotted a group of soldiers on motorcycles in the distance. Ria quickly signaled for us to take cover, and we dove over the guard rails into a nearby ditch. As we

Chapter 12 "From Armen With Love"

huddled in the ditch, trying to stay quiet and hidden, our eyes scanned the horizon for any signs of danger.

That's when we saw it: a small plane, flying low to the ground. Cake's ears perked up at the sight, and she spoke up excitedly. "At that altitude, it must have just taken off from a nearby airstrip!" Ria and Amara both nodded in agreement, and we all knew what we had to do next.

Chapter 13 "Homeward-Bound"

We followed Cake down the hill and into the woods, moving quickly but quietly toward the direction of the plane. As we navigated through the dense forest, Cake's keen sense of direction and intuition guided us toward the airstrip.

Excitement surged through us as we emerged from the dense woods and caught sight of the airstrip, with the plane parked and ready for departure. We spotted several figures moving around it, and we knew we had to act fast. Crouching behind some bushes, we quickly formulated a plan for how to approach the plane without getting caught. After a few moments, we sprinted down the hill towards our target, our hearts pounding with adrenaline as we drew closer to our goal. However, as we approached, we noticed guard towers nestled behind trees surrounding the strip. "Guard towers," Ria remarked, "We'll have to move quickly."

Hurtling down the hill towards the airstrip, my balance faltered on a loose rock, sending me tumbling toward a soldier on patrol. In a chaotic and jumbled mess, we both careened down the steep incline. Our fall resulted in an awkward position that rendered the soldier unconscious and surprisingly cushioned my impact. As we fell, his weapon discharged, and a bullet hurtled toward a nearby guard tower overlooking the airstrip.

As the shot rang out, we heard a guard scream and watched him tumble over the edge of the tower. Unfortunately, in a stroke of terrible luck, the guard's weapon discharged as he fell, and a bullet struck a pilot who was preparing to take off from the airstrip. The pilot slumped over and crashed into the security hangar, causing a massive explosion as it crash into the airstrips gas line.

The impact of the blast knocked Amara, Ria, and Cake off their feet. They watched in shock as multiple hangars and guard towers were engulfed in flames due to the chain reaction. Ria and Amara stood there, stunned, unable to process the sheer devastation before them. Meanwhile, Cake seemed unaffected by the catastrophic event and quipped, "Well, that solves the guard tower problem." After Amara helped me up, the four of us then dashed towards the single parked plane on the airstrip.

* * *

While we were running towards the plane, the sound of the guards on their motorcycles echoed behind us. My heart was pounding in my chest as we approached the aircraft. Cake rushed towards the cockpit and attempted to start the engine, but it wouldn't budge.

As time was running out, the guards were closing in on us. Without hesitation, Ria leaped onto the tail of the plane, poised to fire the tail gun. The revving of their engines grew louder as they approached.

Suddenly, the engine roared to life, and the plane began to move. We were hurtling down the runway with the guards hot on our heels. Ria fired the tail gun, hitting one of the motorcycles and causing it to spin out of control.

We took off, and I looked back and saw the guards in hot pursuit. They were firing their weapons, but we were too high for their shots to hit us.

While flying away from the airstrip, the sound of other planes roaring to life filled the sky. Cake displayed expertise in maneuvering our stolen aircraft, deftly evading enemy fire, and performing daring aerial acrobatics while engaging in dogfights with other planes.

Just when I thought things couldn't get any worse, a massive airship loomed in the distance, emerging from the clouds with a dark and ominous presence. 'That's the biggest airship I've ever seen,' Ria said, her voice tense with apprehension.

"It's also the most heavily armed," Cake added, her eyes fixed on the advancing airship.

As we closed in on the airship, the enemy planes intensified their attacks. Ria manned the tail gun, firing round after round at the incoming planes. But her gun jammed, and she cursed under her breath.

"I got this," Amara said, pulling out her revolver and taking aim at one of the approaching planes. She fired a shot, and the pilot slumped forward, sending the plane spiraling out of control.

With Amara's expert marksmanship and Cake's skillful piloting, and Ria eventually managing to unjam the gun and to join the fray, we were able to take down several more planes. However, the airship was still approaching, and its cannons were aimed directly at us.

The airship opened fire, and we were jolted by the impact of the exploding shells. Ria fired desperately at the oncoming barrage, but it seemed futile. We were outgunned and outmatched.

Amara's voice echoed through the plane as she cried out, "I've got an opening!" With precision, she steadied her aim and fired a shot from her revolver, striking the airship's pilot. As the aircraft careened off course, We watched in awe as the massive ship plummeted toward the forest below, exploding on impact.

We soared away from the burning wreckage of the airship, the flames casting a fiery glow across the sky. As we flew into the sunset, Ria turned to Amara and remarked, "I guess you're not rusty anymore."

Amara grinned and replied, "Yep, I guess not. I've got him to thank," gesturing towards me.

Ria smiled warmly and said, "I'm glad you're back, Amara. I really am." She climbed out of the tail gun and hugged her tightly.

As we ascended into the clouds, the warmth of the setting sun on our faces, I couldn't help but feel a sense of relief that I was finally going to be headed home. However, the weight of the looming Lilith's problem settled heavily on me. I took solace in the fact that I had Amara by my side, and I knew that with her, there was nothing we couldn't face together.

The sky was calming, and a gentle breeze blew over us as I drifted off to sleep. Amara cuddled up to me as she noticed me nodding off. My dream was surreal, and I struggled to decipher its meaning. I saw a flower growing in the shade of a tree atop a hill, and it endured through changing seasons. However, a deer appeared during a storm and ate the flower, causing a branch from the tree to fall and kill the deer. The tree began to wither and look diseased, but a little flower grew at its base. The tree eventually grew bigger, covered in many flowers, and animals and plants thrived under its shade.

As my dream faded away, darkness took over, and Lilith appeared on the ground with pinkish-red eyes looking up at the void. Her thoughts echoed in the void, "I will find you, I love you, where are you? Do you love me? I'm sorry, forgive me. I'm sorry. Why won't you listen? I will kill you." As I approached Lilith, I noticed her pupils were gone, her eyes were blank, and her floppy ears were distorted. She turned over to me and lunged, and a gunshot rang out. I realized I was the one who fired it as she collapsed to the ground. She impaled me with her now sharp claws, and I looked down in shock as she reverted to her old self, saying "thank you" as she died. I stumbled back and fell into the void, feeling a sense of peace.

Amara shook me awake, and I opened my eyes to find that we were at the airstrip overlooking New Colombia - we were finally home. Ria and Cake were celebrating, feeling proud of what they had accomplished, but their celebrations were tinged with sadness as they had to leave to go home. We stepped out of the biplane and bid our farewells to Ria and Cake. I thanked them both from the bottom of my heart, and Ria and Amara exchanged words of gratitude toward each other.

Amara gave Ria her prized revolver, and Ria knew what it meant. Tears filled Ria's eyes as she hugged Amara tightly, and then she handed her a can of "RapidHeal." "I know you're out now, but you never know when you'll need this," Ria said. She then told Amara to take care of me and not drift apart as they did.

   Amara responded by giving Ria a quick kiss and reminding her to take care of Cake.

   Playfully, Cake complained, "Ria, you're not taking care of me." Ria

Chapter 13 "Homeward-Bound"

blushed and swooped up Cake, kissing her with such fervor that the poor girl seemed on the verge of exploding into a bloody mess.

As Ria and Cake took off into the sunset, waving their goodbyes, Amara turned to me with eyes glinting like a predator and tackled me to the ground. She hugged and kissed me while we gazed up at the sun. As much as I wanted to stay in that moment forever, I knew we had to stop Lilith if she hadn't already been stopped. So we made our way to the New Colombia central police station. Luckily, we managed to hitch a ride with my former boss, Sal, who recognized me on the side of the road trying to signal down people like a cash-for-gold sign wielder.

Sal, a trans raccoon girl with grayish-white hair and orange eyes, was wearing a gray crop top, black shorts, and a crucifix necklace. Her big, fluffy raccoon tail flicked up in excitement as she saw me, her eyes gleaming with surprise. Her partner, a brown long-haired, brown-skinned woman with freckles, was asleep in the front seat. Amara and I rode in the back, ready to face whatever awaited us in New Colombia. As we entered Sal's car, she greeted us with a warm smile and a pat on the head. She went on to explain to me that I had been marked as a missing person for over six months, and everyone had presumed me dead. I couldn't believe it, and Sal jokingly talked about redacting the in-memoriam from the graphic novel. I then told her no, she should keep it; we probably still needed it.

After sharing my journey to this point, Sal seemed to believe me once I showed her my healed scars and wounds. I asked if she had any contact with Lilith, and she responded with a no. Lilith had gone hysterical after my disappearance and was looking everywhere for me.

I asked Sal if the police had investigated Lilith after my disappearance. She shook her head and replied, "No, you know how incompetent New

Colombia's police force is. Why bother with them?" I explained that the police were our only option to stop Lilith. Sal agreed but warned us that if that failed - which it probably would - she had some friends who could assist us. All we needed to do was call her. Upon arriving at the police station, Sal bid us farewell, wished us luck, and we made our way to the entrance.

The New Colombia Central Police Building loomed large, with its dimly lit exterior illuminated by only a pair of street lamps. Upon entering, we were greeted by a blonde-haired, blue-eyed policewoman sitting behind the front desk. I explained everything to her - how Lilith was the serial killer who had attempted to kill me. However, to my surprise, the officer didn't believe me and pointed out that they had already arrested a middle-aged wolf-man for the crimes. Despite his unassuming appearance, I insisted that it was Lilith who was responsible for my disappearance.

The officer demanded proof, but all I had were my healed scars from my journey. She dismissed them and called over a male officer, who joined in the laughter at our ridiculous story. Frustrated, I raised my voice in protest, telling them that I was a missing person and should have been in the system. The officers checked but found no record of me being marked as one. Eventually, the officers threatened to arrest us for wasting their time if we didn't leave the premises.

Though disheartened, we refused to give up and decided to ride the bus to every station we could find, only to be met with the same disbelief and rejection. In desperation, we reached out to Sal and asked for her help to contact her friends. They arrived clad in black with masks of various colors, wielding bats and zip ties adorned with flags and causes. Two of them were humanoid, one with a wolf tail and the other with a fox tail, while the human among them wore a witch's hat covering her

Chapter 13 "Homeward-Bound"

pink hair and a mask over her face. As we drove towards Lilith's house, the girl in the witch's hat asked me for directions, though I wished she would use GPS instead.

Upon arrival, they handed us masks, weapons, and zip ties, and we set out on our search for Lilith. The one in the witch's hat approached the door and signaled for one person to stand on the other side of it. She counted down with her hand before kicking it down, revealing the big boots she was wearing. They stormed in, tearing apart the house in search of Lilith. Amara followed behind as they flipped over furniture, checked cabinets and closets, and left no stone unturned. They even searched the attic and her bedroom, but Lilith was nowhere to be found. After all that effort, we decided to wait for Lilith to come back home, but days went by, and there was no sign of her.

We were at a loss for what to do next, but Sal's friends had to leave. We thanked them for their help, although they did take a few appliances without permission. I allowed it, feeling petty and vengeful at the moment. As they drove away in their black van, Amara sat beside me, sensing my disappointment and offering her favorite pastime - cuddling me. I couldn't help but wonder if Lilith had fled and was on the run, afraid that I would reveal her secret. While this thought brought some comfort, it did not provide closure. I told Amara that I needed to go home and gather some of my belongings, my voice tinged with both sadness and hopefulness.

Chapter 14 "Home Sweet Home"

Upon arriving at the house, I explained to Amara that I needed some time alone to process the sudden rush of memories that returning home would bring. She was understanding and agreed to wait outside, assuring me that she was there if I needed any help. Grateful for her unwavering support, I entered the house, bracing myself for the emotional rollercoaster that lay ahead.

As I moved from room to room, I gathered my belongings while reflecting on the times I spent with Lilith. I collected my photos, leaving behind those featuring her, and packed my entertainment center, remembering the countless hours we spent gaming and watching movies together.

Heading upstairs, I grabbed some clothing, including a few questionable cosplay outfits that I knew I wouldn't be wearing again, and searched for my favorite bomber jacket. However, I couldn't find it, along with a cherished picture of myself that Lilith had taken. I wondered if she had taken them and when. Approaching the nightstand, I noticed a drop of water and looked up to find a gaping hole in the ceiling and a soaking-wet carpet. Cursing my luck, I took a few steps forward and suddenly plummeted through the floor, landing hard in the basement.

As I regained my senses, I took in the surrounding environment. The walls were covered in dried blood and scrawled messages like "I love him" and "Where is he? Find him." My gaze then fell upon Lilith, who lay motionless on a couch, staring blankly at the ceiling while clutching the missing picture of me in my bomber jacket.

* * *

Despite Lilith's appearance being lifeless, I checked her pulse and was surprised to find that she was still barely clinging to life. Feeling uneasy and unsettled, I gathered my belongings from where I had stumbled and made my way toward the basement's exit. However, when I reached the door, I realized that it was jammed shut, preventing me from leaving. As I struggled to open it, a chilling voice emanated from the basement," Who's there?".

My heart began to race as I turned to find Lilith standing at the foot of the stairs, her eyes fixed on me with an eerie intensity. With a sense of foreboding, I watched as she began to ascend the stairs toward me. Frantically trying to open the door, I could feel my panic escalating with each passing moment. As Lilith neared the top of the staircase, my heart pounded harder than it ever had before, and my attempts to force the door open became even more frantic.

In an instant, my world turned upside down as I fell through the stairs, my body firmly wedged in the splintered wood. My heart racing, I looked up to see Lilith slowly approaching, her ghostly appearance causing my skin to go cold. I could see every detail of her inner workings - her muscles, bones, and even eyeballs - visible beneath her translucent skin. Fear gripped me as I realized the severity of my situation, and I screamed for Amara to come to my aid while frantically trying to free myself. As Lilith drew nearer, looming over me, she crouched down to examine me with a disturbing curiosity.

Her eyes scanned me, revealing the blood vessels on the sides, and I couldn't help but observe the intricate movement of her facial and arm muscles as she adorned two black bracelets. As she fastened them, her skin returned to its normal pale state, and a wicked smile spread across her face, sending shivers down my spine.

"It's you," she whispered, her hot, rotting breath hitting my face as she slowly licked my cheek. I struggled harder to break free, As her grip tightened around my shoulders. "I missed you," she continued, tears streaming down her face.

My heart raced as I trembled with fear, desperately trying to reason with her. However, her words only added to my growing sense of terror. "There's no need to be afraid," she said soothingly, attempting to calm me down. "I was just waking from hibernation. My skin naturally does that. I haven't eaten in a while because I really missed you. But now that you're back, I can finally eat again." Her words only served to deepen my unease as I wondered what she meant by "eat again." My mind raced with possibilities, none of which were particularly reassuring.

My heart was beating out of my chest as I realized the gravity of the situation. I needed help, and I needed it now. "Amara!" I screamed, hoping that she could hear me. "Amara, where are you?"

With inhuman strength, Lilith pressed down on my shoulders, forcing me through the stairs. "I won't make the same mistake and drive you away. This way, we can be together forever," she declared as I landed on the basement floor, disoriented. Lilith descended the stairs, shouting, "I won't kill you, but I'll make sure you never leave!" Despite my fear, I cried out again for Amara, this time more bloodcurdling. However, Lilith demanded, "Who do you keep calling for?" I answer her with fear and Defiance, I responded, "My girlfriend."

Lilith paused at the edge of the stairs, shocked and dazed. "I know what you are. We can never be together. You need help!" I continued, "What am I, Jonathan?" Lilith responded, tears streaming down her face. "You're an alien, and you and your sister Lila have eaten countless people. You're a monster," I replied. Her eyes widened before she responded, "Lila? That's impossible!"

"How did you get there?" Lilith asked, her curiosity piqued. I explained how I ended up on the abandoned island and met her sister. Her face lit up with a smile as she exclaimed, "She's alive!" But her joy was short-lived as she turned to me. "She must have seen the same thing I saw in you for you not to be dead," she said, tears streaming down her face. "Please love me again," she pleaded, her voice turning menacing. "Lilith, please," I begged, trying to inch away.

"You don't love me, but I still love you, and I'm going to make you love me," she declared, slowly approaching me. "Without you, I have nothing. Please, love me. I don't want to have to do this."

I protested that I could never love her like this, no matter what she did to me. "You need help. This isn't you," I spat out, hoping to reason with her.

With a firm grip on my leg, she pulled me closer to her, flipping me over in the process. Tears streamed down her face as she pleaded, "Please, love me." But I couldn't comply. It wasn't until she revealed her sharp fangs that I realized too late what she intended to do. As she sank her teeth into my shoulder, breaking the skin, I screamed in horror. The pain was excruciating as she repeated the action, biting into my other shoulder, and I cried out again. "I'm sorry," she said calmly, but the damage was already done. "Please, Lilith," I screamed in agony. "Love me," she responded, but I couldn't reciprocate her feelings.

"I'll make this quick," she said coldly as she scratched my face, causing blood to flow from the fresh wound, which she then licked off cleanly. She tore through my shirt, exposing my chest, before attempting to bite my abdomen. In agony, I asked her what she planned to do with me, and she replied, "I'll consume every part of you, leaving not a drop of blood or bone, so that we can become one."

Suddenly, Amara charged at Lilith with full force, catching her off guard and slamming her into the drywall, which crumbled under the impact. She then helped me up and apologized profusely for not checking on me earlier, explaining that she had to deal with a suspicious cop outside who thought she was robbing the house. Although Amara heard me yelling, she couldn't come to my aid since the cop had her at gunpoint. However, she managed to disable him by throwing a handful of dirt in his eyes.

As Lilith got back on her feet and pursued us, we quickly made our way to the stairs. "So, you replaced me with her?" Lilith exclaimed. "I'll tear her apart!" We dashed out of the front door and tried to explain to the cop what was happening, but he aimed his gun at us. We fled as Lilith emerged from the house, and the officer ordered her to stop. But with her inhuman strength, Lilith punched through the officer's body, causing him to collapse to the ground. Backup arrived, and they opened fire on us, prompting Amara and me to dive into the squad car of the fallen officer as bullets riddled the front of the house.

* * *

As the dust settled, Lilith stood unfazed by the gunfire. She tore the bullet-ridden door off its hinges and hurled it at a female officer, creating a deafening cracking sound upon impact. I couldn't believe what I was witnessing. Lilith was demonstrating impossible feats of strength that left me baffled. The officer's partner, stunned by the display of strength, gathered the courage to rush Lilith in a blind rage and fired his weapon while she was distracted. We tried to pull away in the squad car but heard a blood-curdling scream and the sound of bones cracking as we drove off, leaving the chaos behind. Lilith shouted as we drove away, "Stop running! There's no escaping from love!".

* * *

We thought we were in the clear, but Lilith quickly caught up to us in the backups patrol car. She relentlessly rammed the back of our car as we sped through the suburbs, narrowly avoiding an in-ground pool as we crashed through a backyard fence. We entered the highway, but Lilith remained hot on our tail, weaving through traffic as we dodged in and out. We were fast approaching a line of completely stopped traffic ahead. Amara knew she had to do something drastic to lose Lilith, so she made the risky decision to drive into oncoming traffic.

    I trusted Amara and gave her a reassuring hand on the shoulder as we crossed the median to the other side. Lilith followed closely behind, but Amara kept weaving and dodging through traffic with ease. She managed to squeeze the car between two semi-trucks before crossing back over the median.

Suddenly, Lilith's car clipped a semi-truck, causing it to spin out of control and fly over the highway before crashing into a fiery explosion. At first, I felt relieved that the danger was over, but my relief was short-lived when I saw Lilith in the rearview mirror. She had commandeered a semi-truck and was causing massive deadly accidents to catch up with us. In an attempt to evade her and prevent any more innocent people from being hurt, Amara drove off the next exit and headed towards the city.

* * *

Lilith continued to chase us, carelessly crashing into parked cars as we fled. In a split-second decision, Amara took us on a detour through an old, abandoned mall. We crashed through the glass entrance and jumped from the upper floor to the bottom floor, causing significant damage to the car's suspension and rendering it useless. With Lilith hot on our heels, we scrambled out of the disabled vehicle and ran for our lives.

As Lilith attempted to jump the truck from the top floor, it landed awkwardly and crashed through old, abandoned kiosks and the disabled squad car, causing a massive explosion that shook the entire mall. We didn't look back and kept running until we reached a police station, hoping to find help.

Upon arriving, I explained the situation to the police officer on duty, who happened to be the same cop we had encountered before. She immediately ordered our arrest for wasting police time, but just as she was about to handcuff us, Lilith burst through the door, her clothes burnt, her hair disheveled, and her skin bearing minor scrapes and bruises. Her black arm bracelets were loose at the moment, and my

Chapter 14 "Home Sweet Home"

brain struggled to remember what Lila had said about them.

Lilith sniffed the air until she caught a particular scent and locked eyes with me. The female officer asked if she was the one, and I confirmed her suspicion. The officers ordered Lilith to freeze, but she ignored them and began approaching me slowly and menacingly. As she got closer, I had an epiphany and remembered that the bracelets granted her indestructibility. I yelled at the officers to remove the black bracelets, hoping it would help.

Backup arrived just as Lilith approached us, and they opened fire on her with shotguns. Despite being hit by several rounds, Lilith remained unfazed and continued walking towards us. Amid the chaos, Amara and I made a run for the back of the police station and took the stairs up to the roof. As we ascended, the sound of screams suddenly turned into deafening silence.

***

We finally reached the rooftop after what felt like an eternity, hoping that the officers had managed to stop Lilith. We were cornered with nowhere to go, waiting with bated breath. It was quiet for a while until the door to the roof burst open, and Lilith emerged, gripping two officers by their necks. With a menacing look on her face, she flung one officer towards us, sending him hurtling over the edge of the roof. Without hesitation, she then launched the second officer toward the ground, where he groaned upon impact. As Lilith charged towards us, Amara swiftly grabbed my hand and pulled me away, leaping off the roof and soaring through the air towards a nearby building. At that moment, time seemed to slow down as we watched the window in front of us grow closer and closer.

As we crashed through the window, Lilith's disdainful expression burned into my mind. It was clear that Amara was injured as she struggled to stand up, and I was also in pain - my shoulder had dislocated, and my ankle felt broken. Looking back at the shattered window we had jumped through, we saw Lilith preparing to jump after us. The sight horrified both of us. As she charged toward us with reckless abandon, Lilith's determination was palpable. However, just as she launched herself into the air, the downed officer threw dirt in her eyes, momentarily blinding her.

The distraction caused her to overshoot her target, and she collided with the side of the building. As she tumbled down the side of the structure, her bracelets came loose, flew through the window, and clattered to the ground beside us with a resounding metallic thud.

Despite the chaos that had just occurred, Amara managed to gather her wits and stand up. She limped over to me, using the wall to keep herself steady, and offered a sincere apology. She then popped my dislocated shoulder back into place, causing me to cry out in pain. After examining my ankle, which was also broken, she prepared herself and warned me before forcefully snapping it back into place with an audible crack.

To our amazement, Amara produced a can of "RapidHeal" that she used to treat all of our injuries. The spray had an immediate effect, and our wounds, including my ankle and shoulder injuries, began to heal rapidly. We winced as the spray stung with extreme sharpness, but soon we were able to use our limbs again without pain.

"I was saving that for a rainy day," Amara said with a wry smile. "I guess this was that rainy day."

"Ria's intuition never fails to impress me," Amara said, looking up and smiling.

Together, we approached the window and looked down at the alley below, where Lilith lay crumpled and motionless. After examining the bracelets, I placed them in my pocket, and we descended into the elevator. We stepped outside the apartment complex to find a swarm of police officers surrounding the alley. We were questioned, and my heart sank when I received confirmation that Lilith was dead.

Chapter 15 "A Long Journey Nowhere"

The officer unzipped the body bag, revealing Lilith's peaceful face. Suddenly, she stirred, slowly opening her eyes and fixing her gaze on me. The officer backed away, holding her gun holster, and goosebumps covered my body as cold sweat formed on my skin. But those were not the same eyes that had chased us moments before; they belonged to the Lilith I had first met, the Lilith I loved.

"Keep those away from me," she pleaded, gesturing to the bracelets. "Let me die. You and I both know I deserve this."

"What happened, Lilith?" I asked, my voice trembling.

"I gave in to temptation," she admitted. "After the first night we met, I was able to suppress my desire for two years because of you. But one night, two men attacked me, and I bit one of them. As soon as their blood hit my tongue, I went into a frenzy. From then on, I couldn't resist, but I tried."

"I wish I could have fought harder for you," She said, my heart breaking.

"Why didn't you say something, Lilith? I could have helped you!"

"I'm a monster, and I would only have ended up hurting you."

Tears streamed down my face as I uttered the words, "This is my fault. I should have gotten you help the moment I came home and saw you that night."

"Don't you dare blame yourself," Lilith yelled, tears streaming down her face. "Even as I'm dying, I'm still hurting you. Please, don't let me hurt you anymore. Let me go," she pleaded.

"Lilith" I responded calmly

"I'm sorry for everything I put you through, and I hope that someday you'll find it in your heart to forgive me," Lilith said, tears streaming down her face.

"I forgive you for what you did to me, but not for what you did to others," I replied.

"Thank you, Jon," she said, her voice shaking with emotion. "I never deserved you." She then turned towards Amara, her eyes pleading with her. "Please don't take love for granted as I did. Give him the world. Don't let your love go on a long journey nowhere. Go somewhere together and keep the flame of love alive."

Lilith turned to me, her skin Dulling.

"Jon, could you do me a favor?" she weakly asked.

"What is it?" I replied.

"Cast those bracelets into the ocean. That's where they belong."

"Okay," I said.

Then, Lilith reached out her hands to me. "Let me die in your arms," she said.

I hesitated, searching for guidance from Amara. She nodded, tears welling up in her eyes. I handed her the bracelets and knelt down to hold Lilith in my arms. As she gradually slipped away, she placed an arm on my chest and whispered, "I love you." Her eyes dimmed, and her body grew limp.

I cradled Lilith's motionless body, memories of our times together flooded my mind, filling me with regret. If only I had been aware of her struggle, I could have helped her. I could have saved her if she had only confided in me. But then Amara placed her hands on my shoulders, her weight bearing down on me, and I knew it was time to let go.

When we walked away from the scene, I expressed my gratitude to the officer for allowing me to do what I needed to do. She then apologized for the way she treated us asking if we need anything to just call.

With Amara by my side, I was filled with a mix of emotions. As we made our way down the lively sidewalk, I couldn't help but reminisce about the day I first met her and the bracelets that now sat in my hand.

Despite feeling sadness for Lilith's fate, I am no longer haunted by regret. Hope and joy for the future fill me, and I share my aspirations with Amara as we reach the riverfront and lean on the railing, gazing out at the ocean. She dreams of becoming a jazz musician and using her stolen riches to buy a house and start a family with me. Meanwhile, I plan to continue working on Sal's novel and perhaps even start my own graphic novel. When she asks what my graphic novel will be about, I suggest a story about a world-class gentlewoman thief. She replies with a smile, "I could help you with that."

We stood together at the riverfront for a while, gazing at the sun setting and taking in the serene moment's sights and sounds. I held the bracelets in my hand, contemplating their significance, and then closed my eyes and tossed them into the ocean. As I watched them sink to the bottom, an intense wave of emotion overcame me, and tears welled up in my eyes.

Sensing my sorrow, Amara pulled me in for a kiss, and I felt an overwhelming rush of love like never before. All the positive feelings in the world flooded my soul, and my eyes were clear of tears. The universe around us seemed more beautiful than ever before.

It felt as though Amara had been holding back a lifetime of love, and I was swept away by her passion. Suddenly, the world faded around us, and we found ourselves floating through the cosmos, surrounded by stars. We saw the vastness of the universe, and for a moment, time stood still.

As we returned to the riverfront, I couldn't help but wonder if it had all been a dream.

Later on, we made our way to a payphone and reached out to my boss, asking if she could provide us with a place to stay. As I needed a roof over my head, my boss welcomed us into her home without hesitation. She showed us to the guest room, which had beige walls, a queen-size bed, and a shelf with a CRT Television. Sal was filled with excitement as we settled into the cozy space.

As we were getting comfortable, my boss introduced us to her roommate, Lilly, a humanoid pale-skinned blonde dog girl with big floppy golden retriever ears and a golden retriever tail. Lilly was wearing a big loose-fitting gray graphic hoodie and wagging her tail in excitement. Kelly, my boss's partner, who was in the car when we went to the police station, also introduced herself before heading off to bed. They assured us that if we needed anything, we could call for them.

After turning off the lights, the room was cast in a soothing dark and light purple light from the lamp. We went to "**Sleep**" like good responsible adults, with Amara holding me close after. As we settled in for the night, she reached for the stereo and selected a smooth jazz track that held a special significance to her: a song she had composed many years ago but had never before shared with anyone. With the gentle melody filling the room, I couldn't help but express my love for her. She returned my feelings with equal passion, drawing me near and holding me in a loving embrace until we fell asleep.

As I dozed off, the sweet melody of Amara's jazz tune lingered in my mind, and I envisioned Lilith's bracelets sinking deeper and deeper into the beautiful blue ocean full of life.

Chapter 15 "A Long Journey Nowhere"

Verse 1:
   The night is young, the stars are bright
   I'm feeling lost in the city lights

But then I see you, my heart takes flight
   It's like we're the only ones in sight

Chorus:
   This moment feels so right

With you here by my side
I never want to say goodbye
Cause I love you

Verse 2:
    The music plays, the saxophone cries
    It's like the rhythm of our lives
    Our souls entwine, we're in paradise
    I'll cherish this moment all my life

Chorus:
    This moment feels so right
    With you here by my side

I never want to say goodbye
    Cause I love you

Bridge:
    I never thought I'd find someone
    Who makes my heart beat like a drum
    But now I know that you're the one
    I'll love you till the end of time

Chorus:
    This moment feels so right
    With you here by my side
    I never want to say goodbye
    Cause I love you

Outro:
   I'll always hold you close and true
   My love for you will never be through
   And with every breath, I'll say anew

I love you.

Saxophone solo
   Chorus:
   This moment feels so right

Chapter 15 "A Long Journey Nowhere"

With you here by my side
I never want to say goodbye
Cause I love you.

It was a peaceful moment, watching them find their final resting place

END

Thank you!

Dear Reader,

Thank you so much for reading my debut book. Your support means everything to me, and I hope that the story has resonated with you. If you enjoyed the book, I would be grateful if you could share it with others by purchasing a physical copy or renting a digital ebook on the Internet Archive. Your support would mean the world to me.

However, if the book did not meet your expectations, I am truly sorry for any disappointment caused. I promise to continue to hone my craft and strive to create better stories that will resonate with you in the future. If you have any feedback or thoughts on the book, please do not hesitate to reach out to me at **aurorablazeboomentertainment@gmail.com**. Your reviews would also be greatly appreciated.

Once again, thank you for your support, and I hope to continue to provide you with stories that captivate your imagination.

Warm regards,
Aurora Blaze

Ingram Content Group UK Ltd.
Milton Keynes UK
UKHW050259090523
421437UK00004B/79

Dear Readers

While my reasons for publishing a book are never frivolous, some of the stories have a more lighthearted tone overall than others. This story is one of the more lighthearted.

My initial idea for writing this book has been with me for a few years, but I didn't feel the real push to write it until a time of international crisis in 2020.

It got me thinking back on some of the hardest times in my personal life, when key lifesavers of mine have been smiles, laughter, and the encouragement to hold on to hope.

At whatever time or season you're reading this book, whether purely for leisure or because you're in need of hope and inspiration, may the story add a good dose of lightness to your heart.

~ *Nadine*

"A cheerful heart is a good medicine"
Proverbs 17:22, ASV

Nadine. A French name, meaning, "hope."

With her lifelong passion for life-enriching fiction, Nadine C. Keels enjoys reading and writing everything from short stories to novels. Her fiction works include *Love Unfeigned* and *The Movement of Crowns Series*, and select pieces of her lyrical poetry can be found on her spoken word album, *Hope. Lyricized.* Through her books and her blog (Prismatic Prospects), Nadine aims to spark hope and inspiration in as many people as she is privileged to reach.

Books by Nadine C. Keels

Movement of Crowns Series
The Movement of Crowns
The Movement of Rings
The Movement of Kings

Crowns Legacy Series
Reviving the Commander
Embracing the Outcast

Eubeltic Realm Series
Eubeltic Descent
Eubeltic Quest
Eubeltic Virtue

For Every Love: Three Romantic Reads
Realizing Love: Three Romantic Reads
Inspiring Love: Three Romantic Reads
Yella's Prayers
World of the Innocent

Kiss and Telle?

Chapter One

"Welp. We might as well, 'Telle."

With that suggestion directed her way and the accompanying hand held out to her, Chantelle Jackson let her gaze move from the proffered hand and up into the eyes of Dennis Lawson.

Those brown eyes sparkled down at her from behind a pair of black-framed glasses. Eyes that were full of life and so much…fun.

Chantelle resisted the niggling urge to let a sigh loose. *Fun.*

Here she was, the maid of honor sitting at the now nearly empty head table at the Saturday evening wedding reception of two of her best friends. The halter neck, garnet red gown she had on was one of the most elegant garments that had ever graced her wide-shouldered, gently curved form, the flow of fabric accommodating her few extra pounds in such a way that she'd had no need for extra shapewear or the extra effort to avoid breathing all day. She'd recently forgone her usual abundance of long braids to wear only her thick, natural hair for a while, and today she wore a flower above her ear, adding a burst of color to her dark billow of hair. It was the closest she would come to wearing a tiara on this occasion, since she wasn't the bride, but the blossom in her hair still made her feel queenly.

That is, she'd felt queenly for most of the day. Queenly and vibrant and full of anticipation, going about her bridesmaid duties with a light step in her fine dress, on the lookout for the potential moment when she'd know that Dennis had taken notice.

There he was, the best man at the wedding reception of two of their best friends, the jacket of his black tuxedo presently missing as he stood there in a garnet cummerbund and matching bowtie that flashed in red against the white of his shirt. His black hair was styled in a fresh buzz cut with a hint of waves on top. He looked smart and snazzy, the essence of his usual swagger there. Swagger he wore like no other geek-at-heart on the planet could.

Chantelle had wanted this swaggering and smart geek-at-heart to take notice of her today, in a way he apparently hadn't in any of the previous years of their decade-long friendship. Perhaps Chantelle had put too much trust in her hopeless yet hopeful romanticism, imagining that, regardless of the fact that Dennis had seen her all dressed up before, the special love in the air at the nuptials of Alexis

Prescott—now Alexis Simmons—and Arthur Simmons would influence Dennis and finally give him ideas. Ideas that would lead to something more intimate than the fun in his eyes.

But, nope. Couples had joined the bride and groom out on the floor to dance to the jazzy Christmas music from the live band playing in the reception hall, led by Arthur's older brother, a vocalist who also played the guitar. (Leave it to Alexis and Arthur to choose a Yuletide theme for their spring wedding, a choice that only those two lovebirds fully understood. Yes, the new Mr. and Mrs. were their own kind of geeks too, bless their hearts.) Chantelle had done most of her hostessing, Dennis had delivered the main reception speech and proposed the toast, and the two of them were now free to join the others out on the floor, but there was no humble and gentlemanly "May I have this dance?" from Dennis. There wasn't a dashing request tinged with longing, a "Would you do me the honor?" to the maid of honor.

Instead, Dennis suggested that Chantelle dance with him because they were here, there was music, and other people were dancing, so, welp, the two of them might as well.

At that moment, Chantelle no longer felt so queenly. She felt comfortable, like the effortless, trouble-free, comfortable choice to be Dennis's dance partner at a party. Granted, her twinge of disappointment wasn't a particularly comfortable one, but that wasn't anyone's business but her own.

No use letting on.

Chantelle remained seated at the table and smiled a mild challenge up at Dennis until she meant both the challenge and the smile. "Don't know if I can manage it, best man. Been a long day. My puppies are yipping."

Dennis didn't back away. "One hundred percent your fault." He dropped his outstretched hand and surprised Chantelle by getting down, kneeling near her chair.

Gasp! Dennis was getting down on one knee on an evening when so much love was in the air. As Chantelle certainly hadn't imagined quite this far, she could hardly control the spinning of her wits for a second. But it was only a second, as the outdated language that scrambled through her imagination involved a gentleman asking for a lady's hand, not a gentleman asking for a lady's foot.

Or, as Dennis ordered her more so than he asked her: "Gimme your foot."

Chantelle shifted her sitting position, scooting her yipping puppies away from him. "Beg your pardon?"

"Your foot. Give it here. And give the other one here too, while you're at it. Chop-chop."

Chantelle didn't chop-chop. She took her time before scooting back in Dennis's direction, and he waited until she tugged her skirt to lift the hem of her gown above her ankle and curiously lifted one of her feet a degree from the floor.

Belying his brash bossiness, Dennis's touch was tender as he began to remove one of Chantelle's high-heeled shoes. "If you would opt for less torturous ways to decorate your feet than all of these restrictive straps attached to stilts that wreak havoc on your arches," Dennis scolded, grinning as he did so, "your precious pups wouldn't yip so much."

Chantelle wiggled her toes with the relief of it all once she was free from the painful prettiness of her shoes, and after Dennis stowed the heels away under the table, he stood back up, holding his hand out to Chantelle. She accepted it this time, staring down at their fingers coming together, Dennis's skin a deeper brown than hers, although the sun would slow-toast her into a darker tone as spring moved into summer.

"Humph. 'We might as well,'" Chantelle repeated with a shake of her head once she and Dennis were out on the dance floor, gliding and swaying to the spirit of Christmas. "Sometimes I wonder if you've got a single romantic cell in that brain of yours."

"No need to wonder about my brain cells. I've got romance coming out of my ears." Dennis nodded toward the newlyweds, over there in the center of the floor. "Those two wouldn't have jumped the broom today if it wasn't for me. You know I'm the one who told Arthur to go for it in the first place, last year. He would've let Lexi get away otherwise."

"Beg your pardon again, but I was the first one who said something about Arthur and Alexis getting together, back in high school. Remember? He resisted it then because he thought it was weird, the idea of dating a friend." Chantelle's voice slowly lowered as the end of her commentary slipped from her mouth. *Dating a friend.*

"He wouldn't have thought it was weird if he hadn't been distracted by that other what's-her-name at the time," Dennis scoffed, as if he couldn't very well recall what's-her-name's name. "Folks who date should be friends, if they can help it."

Chantelle's eyebrows flew up. "You think so?" she blurted before her voice was ready, giving her words a wobble.

If Dennis heard the wobble, he didn't show it. "Absolutely." He shrugged a nonchalant shoulder. "I mean, who'd want to date an enemy? It's already a hassle going out with somebody you like. Why make it even harder on yourself by going out with somebody you can't stand?"

In spite of herself, Chantelle laughed. "Enemies become lovers all the time. Opposites attract, and all that. Besides, from where I'm standing, dating has never looked like much of a hassle for you, Romeo."

"Ah. That's the mark of a master, Chantelephone. Masters of an art make it look easy to folks on the outside looking in." Dennis pulled her nearer to him, until they were virtually cheek to cheek. "And don't call me Romeo. He only got—like, what?—two seconds of bliss with his Juliet before everything tumbled downhill and crashed. That won't be me."

"Oh, no, never you. Never the master." A chortle bounced in Chantelle's throat. "Now, I would pick apart what your deluded definition of 'master' must be in this case, but I prefer to save my breath about rational stuff for people with sense."

"Yeah? Well, if you've been saving your breath with me all these years, you've sure been doing a yakety-yak-yakkin' job of it."

"Says you. But you've no idea how much breath I've saved, Jawbone." Chantelle might have come up with more of a reply than that, but the feel of Dennis's chin barely grazing her temple quieted her for a few heartbeats. She didn't even flinch at the trace of stubble that had crept onto his clean-shaven face over the course of the day, as her increasing relaxation left no room for flinching. And regarding relaxation...

"I've gotta say, though," Chantelle spoke up, "you did quite a job today, keeping Arthur relaxed. Weddings look so dreamy in movies, but whenever I'm at the real thing, the bride floats and cries and/or smiles her way down the aisle, caught up in the happiest day of her life, while the groom is up there clenching his hands and sweating buckets, looking a nanosecond away from passing out. Arthur looked great, though. You must have fed him a steady stream of your bad jokes in the hours beforehand to keep him laughing—at you."

Dennis chuckled. "I can neither confirm nor deny that. But I think only a single guy knows just how daunting the prospect of taking on a whole, entire, real-life *wife* can be. So I reminded Arthur how careful a planner he is, that he wouldn't have asked for Alexis if he wasn't ready to take care of her. I told him not to forget that she'll be taking care of him just as much." He paused to spin Chantelle to the music before he gathered her back to him. "I'm sure you had a lot of encouraging yakety-yak for Lexi."

Chantelle smiled at that. "Any encouragement might have drifted right on past her. She was already in raptures, mostly just needed someone to keep her from sailing off on a glorious cloud with her veil on backwards."

That brought another chuckle from Dennis before he sent Chantelle into a second spin and then tucked her in close.

Chantelle's insides leapt. *Oh, goodness.* This man hadn't any business being such a rhythmic and soulful dance companion for her if none of the romance coming out of his ears had anything to do with her.

Chantelle's eyelids lowered as she melted into the music and her dance companion's familiarity, breathing in the scent of aquatic cologne blended with living Dennis. She'd partnered with him enough times since high school to be aware of how he'd subtly changed over the years. His transition from adolescence to manhood hadn't turned him into a hulking mountain of muscle, but Chantelle was fine with not feeling like she was tucked against something that had been chiseled from a block of granite. Dennis was warm and emanating with verve. He wasn't too wide for her to get her hold a good ways around him whenever they hugged, but the strength about him didn't have to come in bulk for her to feel it, for her to know good and well that she was in the arms of a man.

This man.

The problem was, at some point after their high school days had ended to give way to their college days and beyond, moments like these and plenty of others Chantelle shared with Dennis had been contributing to her ever-intensifying notion that this man might be the only one for her. After high school, the two of them attended the same university in a big city an hour away from their hometown. Chantelle went out with her share of guys, and Dennis did his own dating around, but even while that was happening, Chantelle's friendship with Dennis deepened in college.

Chantelle liked to think that she and Dennis became a new "home" for each other during that phase of their lives. Sure, the two of them still poked and joked and jabbed at each other as much as they ever had, but there was far more to what had grown between them, only growing stronger after they'd graduated and come back to town, reuniting with people they knew and loved, people like Alexis and Arthur.

Chantelle lifted her eyelids to peer thoughtfully over Dennis's shoulder, through other dancing wedding guests and party members, and over at the bride and groom. Alexis and Arthur had officially become a couple a year ago, after their friendship had survived a period of separation. The hopeless and hopeful romantic in Chantelle had been hoping for those two friends of hers even at times when she hadn't been at liberty to say so, and she'd been rooting aloud for them ever since they'd announced they were an item. The way they overcame serious personal obstacles to be together made them such an inspiration to Chantelle.

This time, when the niggling urge came to her, she did let a sigh loose, though not too heavily, not wanting Dennis to ask what was the matter. Would Chantelle still be entertaining what she'd come to feel for Dennis if she hadn't been watching Alexis and Arthur's journey? Had something impressionable in Chantelle gotten the inclination to copy what was working out beautifully for two lovebirds who were close to her, even though Dennis had given no indication of a desire to pursue anything further than friendship with her?

Dear Lord. Help.

"Are your puppies all right?"

Jarred out of her reflections, Chantelle couldn't process Dennis's question near her ear right away. She stalled. "What?"

"I heard that sigh." Dennis's hand at her back gave her a reassuring pat. "We can go sit back down if this is painful."

A delicate smile tugged at Chantelle's lips. Yes, this could indeed be painful. Talking and swaying with Dennis in an atmosphere of matrimonial celebration, springtime's promise, and jazzy Yuletide warmth could be downright agonizing if she thought about it too hard.

So she wasn't going to think about it too hard. At least, she'd stop it for now and save the hard thinking for whenever she'd chronicle this night in her journal.

"Hey," she said. "You told me we might as well, didn't you? Yes? Great. So you're stuck with this." She went so far as to snicker. "You're in dawdle mode. Such wonderful live music in here, and you haven't even dipped me yet." Drawing back a little to look up into the sparkling eyes behind those black-framed glasses, Chantelle tightened her hold on her dance companion's hand and shoulder, issuing a soft and saucy order.

"Chop-chop, best man."

To his credit, Dennis didn't challenge her or take his time. With an indulgent grin at her, he chop-chopped, and Chantelle basked in being so securely held and smoothly dipped into the spirit of Christmas.

Chapter Two

Whoa... Wake up, man.

Dennis shook his head a bit to refocus more of his attention on his driving and the light Sunday traffic around him the next afternoon, but all the head-shaking in the world wasn't going to clear his busy thoughts of Chantelle. Dennis had left service at church early that day to pick up his newlywed charges from their hotel and get them on a plane to fly off to their honeymoon, and Chantelle would be meeting him at his and her favorite sandwich shop, as they'd made plans to have lunch together. Dennis had big news to share with her, and besides that, he wanted to see her anyway. He hadn't been prepared to feel a certain kind of deflation after the wedding, and maybe Chantelle was feeling the same way and could use a boost.

Their tight, four-cornered friendship with Arthur and Alexis had undergone a permanent change, which would become more obvious when the couple got back to town. Of course, the dynamics in their group had already shifted once Arthur and Alexis started dating and then got engaged. Still, a group of four single friends was different from a group of two spouses, a bachelor, and a bachelorette, with one side of the group that would be getting more immersed in married-people stuff as time went on.

Yet, had another change taken place yesterday, one that had to do with more than Arthur and Alexis? Something might have been different when Dennis and Chantelle danced at the wedding reception…

But Dennis had danced with Chantelle more times than he could count, especially considering that their group of friends back in high school attended a lot of their school dances together, except for Alexis, who wasn't as into social events back then. Their core group was bigger at the time, before their friends Isaac, Violet, and Phoebe went their various ways after graduation.

There was nothing more complicated about Dennis partnering with Violet and Phoebe on dance floors as there was about their whole group eating lunches and laughing together at their usual table and spending their daily breaks together in the school commons to snack on shared snacks and to get some reading and studying done while other students around them chatted, hollered, and fooled around. Dancing with Chantelle back then had been as uncomplicated as the rest, so why should the reception last night have been so different?

"Chop-chop, best man."

A shudder went down Dennis's back as he recalled the tone of Chantelle's order along with the complementing look of a slow burn that had shone in her brown eyes. That look might have done more than spark a flame in him if he'd stood there staring, if he hadn't taken immediate action and modified the moment by giving Chantelle the dip she'd demanded.

It wasn't the first time he'd almost gotten lost in Chantelle's eyes, but he couldn't remember her ever looking or sounding quite that way with him before. Had she gone from her usual joking with Dennis to flirting with Dennis?

"*Whoa.*" Dennis tightened his grip on his steering wheel. *Hold up.*

Chantelle Jackson could have any man she wanted, if she wanted. She was brilliant, an absolute numbers geek who'd taken only a year to earn her master's degree at a local college, and then Arthur (with his distinguished and nerdy tech-head self) had been quick about snatching Chantelle up to work in the finance department at the Simmons family's software and web development firm, a business started by Arthur's father and uncle.

Chantelle's brains weren't only technical, as she had a quick and clever sense of humor, and no other woman Dennis had met was a more fitting match to verbally spar with him. Chantelle could dish it as good as she could take it, but she also had a way of affirming Dennis, a way of feeding into his strengths. While they'd been away to earn their undergraduate degrees, regardless of the other women Dennis had gone out with, when he needed someone there he could really talk to, he'd talked to Chantelle.

She'd been the only one there who truly understood how much it was an escape for him, going to college in a different city than the one he'd grown up in. Yes, he'd been on a race to earn a degree that would grant him a lane in the race to success in corporate America, but a huge part of his urgency to go away to college in the first place was on account of his race to bring his childhood household membership to an end. Dennis had been eight years old when his toddler brother, Myles, the child of Dennis's father and stepmother, found a forgotten plate of cookies in their living room late one morning. It was only after the toddler's rapid, severe reaction to his snack that the Lawsons learned Myles was deathly allergic to peanuts.

After Myles didn't make it, his parents were never the same, and Dennis spent the rest of his childhood and adolescence usually feeling like an uninvited guest in his parents' house.

Going off to college gave Dennis a new and needed rush of freedom. Not the freedom to get reckless, as some of his college peers did, but the freedom to do all he could to ensure a stable future for himself. A future where he would belong as more than a guest.

However, even university degrees held no guarantees, and Dennis's post-graduation job search landed him not in corporate America but at an automotive dealership in his hometown, checking brakes and changing tires in the dealership's maintenance shop. Although it was good work that provided necessary services to the public, and Dennis was grateful for the paycheck, the derailment of his career plans still had its frustrations, and as proud as he was of his friends, he'd be lying if he told himself it didn't sting now and then to see Arthur already moving and shaking in software. To see Alexis making a name for herself as an artisan selling handmade items she'd designed and knitted or quilted herself. To see Chantelle sprinting her way down her career path with financial savvy, doing it as a trusted member of Arthur's professional team.

It was Chantelle, though, who sat down with Dennis on a park bench one day after he'd been working in the land of brakes and tires for some months, and out of nowhere, she grabbed Dennis's head and pulled it down, pressing her ear against the hint of black waves on his crown.

"Wha—Chantelle? Girl, what're you doing?"

She didn't answer right away, moving her ear to a different spot on his head, but when she let him go and he straightened up to meet her gaze, she said, "Just wanted to make sure I could hear 'em in there."

Dennis's forehead furrowed as he reached up to run one palm over his hair. "Hear what?"

Chantelle lifted a hand to smooth the wrinkles from his forehead. "Hear your wheels. Turning." She tapped a finger against his temple right above the temple of his glasses. "Same brain as ever, in there. The same mind." Lowering her hand, she then winked at him, of all things. "It's still yours, Dennis. You're the only one who's got yours."

She'd given no preface, and she offered him no more of an explanation, but she didn't have to. The two of them simply sat there for a minute as Dennis caught everything Chantelle meant, and he soaked up every drop of it.

While he could all but feel himself growing inches taller right on that park bench as he sat staring into Chantelle's eyes, he, for the first time, nearly ended up lost in those eyes.

Dennis had long since lost track of how many times it had happened since then, if anyone was counting. He never told anybody about it either way, and he couldn't tell if Chantelle could ever tell, whenever it happened.

Even so, her affirmation about his turning wheels prompted him to pay a new level of attention to the turning: to take stock of his thoughts, his experiences, his learning, his opinions, and his hopes, letting what turned from those wheels gradually turn into writing. He then took what began as journaling for processing and practice, enlisted Arthur's help to create the right website for a new venture, and soon enough, Dennis had a social commentary blog up and running. He named his blog *Lawson Jaws*, having little idea at first that his jawing would strike such a chord with the socially conscious readers who found him.

His blog not only took off but blew up, to the point where he had to switch from checking brakes and changing tires full time to part time, leaving him free to devote more energy to his blogging and his growing audience.

Chantelle took to calling Dennis "Jawson" on the day he launched his blog, and the nickname transitioned to "Jawbone" some time after that. It was another way of affirming Dennis, he knew, even though Chantelle would also use the moniker while poking or joking or jabbing at him.

Still, none of her affirmations or jokes had ever struck him as flirtatious. Not until—

"She doesn't need to waste her time," Dennis mumbled for the benefit of his own hearing as he pulled his car into the parking lot of the sandwich shop, where Chantelle was sure to already be inside, sitting in their normal booth.

That woman who could have any man she wanted wouldn't need to waste time flirting with Dennis, no matter how much he might enjoy it if she did.

But wouldn't it be something if one day when Dennis noticed himself almost getting lost again, Chantelle would wind up noticing it too, but instead of merely noticing what was happening and stopping at "almost," the two of them would go on ahead to get lost together for a while? To get lost and maybe find something?

"Oh, God. For real?" Dennis sent up a questioning petition and let out a groaning sigh to get himself to refocus again as he shoved his cellphone in a pocket of his jacket, climbed out of his car, and brushed off his jeans out of habit. This wasn't any time for jumbled thoughts. He had big news he wanted to share with his friend.

With his *friend*. Chantelle.

Chapter Three

As she checked the time on her cellphone, Chantelle used her free hand to brush at the shoulders of her light, lilac sweater and to smooth her hair leading to the French twist she wore today. Dennis would be arriving at the sandwich shop at any minute.

Chantelle then paused from her primping. What was she primping for? Little good it did to primp for a man who wouldn't be that aware of her appearance.

She then gave her hair a couple of additional pats for good measure. Plenty good it did for a woman to primp for herself.

At any rate, what Chantelle most needed to focus on was getting the rest of her current thoughts down on paper before she lost the flow, and she wanted to get this task out of the way in a hurry. Because, yes, Dennis would be arriving at any minute.

Chantelle snatched up her pen and returned to the open book on the table before her, jotting down notes as fast as she could without sacrificing her handwriting to fuzzy scribbles she would need a detective or a cryptographer to decipher for her later. She'd just flipped a page to get a few final words down when she felt the sudden, blatant drumming of multiple fingertips on her shoulders.

"Whatcha doin', Telephone?"

"Eeep!" Chantelle jumped at the question and whipped her head over to see Dennis coming from around the back of her seat at their usual booth. "Dennis, you—you..." She glanced around the restaurant to see if anyone at any of the other tables had heard her yelp, and she lowered her voice below the lunchtime hubbub. "*Why* would you do that?"

Dennis's brow dramatically scrunched up as he slid into the seat opposite her at the table. "Why would I do what? Ask what you're doing? Because I want to know what you're doing. What're you doing?"

While closing her book, Chantelle shot some version or imitation of a menacing glare across the table. "You're lucky this is the Lord's Day, bucko."

"Oh? Is there any day that isn't the Lord's?" Dennis asked with an over-innocent spread of his hands. "Is there some sort of auxiliary day you never told me about?"

Chantelle concealed a catch in her breath as best as she could. *There's a lot I've never told you. If one main thing is a lot...*

"Are you going to wait for that day to put me in timeout or slap me around," Dennis carried on, "'cause I won't be lucky anymore on Auxiliary Day? It's a shame you're in here threatening people when we're so fresh out of church, sister.

"'Blessed' is the word you should use, by the way. This bucko's blessed. Save calling me 'lucky' for Auxiliary Day or something, although I still wouldn't prefer it, since Lady Luck can be the ficklest chick on the block when she feels like it." He pointed at Chantelle's book. "Anywho. What're you doing? You're gonna make me guess?"

Chantelle jutted her jaw out the precious little that it could jut and hiked up her bottom lip in aggravation and such. Good gravy on a hot baked potato, she wanted to lunge over the table and kiss this guy. Kiss him because it would be the shortest shortcut to come right out and tell him what she'd never told him, and it could also prove to be the shortest shortcut she'd ever found to get the dude to shut up.

Pushing her book to the side, Chantelle set her phone down on top of it with a bit of a thump, as if to thump a case closed. "What do you think I've been doing? I've been waiting for your slow self to get here so that we can get our sandwiches. My tummy tempted me to go to the counter and order without you, but I resisted and gave you a pass for being on Lexi-and-Arthur duty. You got them out of town all right?"

Dennis's finger checked a checkmark in the air. "Signed, sealed, and delivered to their paradise in the tropics, minus the 'delivered' part until they land, text us, and then go black on us." He added with a smirk, "I told Arthur I don't wanna hear squat from them until their week and a half is good and over. No posting a million pics of the beach online either, I said, or I'll report them for spamming everybody. Honeymoons are short enough as it is, without squandering the days on social media. Ain't nobody got time for that. At least honeymooners shouldn't."

"Arthur hardly ever posts pics anyway, Alexis isn't too far ahead of him, and how many honeymoons have you been on to know how they are, smarty-britches? Once brides and grooms are there, maybe the time stretches out."

"Maybe. And if I believe that, I'll bet you've got a one-way ticket to Neptune you want to sell me." Dennis pointed at Chantelle's book again. "What were you doing? You know you could have ordered without me, or ordered for me." He gave his eyebrows a few flashy bounces, dropping his tone to a deeper level than was usual for him. "You know what I like."

Chantelle gave a sarcastic grunt in lieu of a laugh, her instinct trying to ignore the possibility that Dennis's joke may've come off as something a bit other than jokey. "Yeah, your routine meatball sandwich order, extra sauce and parmesan. What if I didn't order that for you because I was hoping you'd break out of your routine and try doing something different now?"

Chantelle didn't like how earnest her question wound up sounding. She also wasn't too wild about the way Dennis sensed her slight shift in attitude, she could tell.

He didn't miss a beat, his joking tone easing off. "Not everybody wants to go searching around for something different, something else, when they're so into what they already know."

Chantelle stared at Dennis for an unnerving moment. What exactly were they talking about, here?

Right. Sandwiches.

She cleared her throat. "You know, we get together a lot to stuff our faces, but we really should get back to jogging."

Dennis only sat there for a second, and then he shook his head. Or rather, he shook himself in general. "What do you mean, 'back' to jogging? Not another 5-million-mile run like that other one you wheedled me into."

"That was a 5K run. It was for charity, it was quite a while ago, and no, we don't have to jog for that long a distance every time. But we should jog." Chantelle patted at her middle, under the table. "I've put on a little more than I'm okay with, these past months."

"Welp. As they say, more to love. I'm too skinny a guy to be getting love handles, but I'm starting to get them anyway, and you haven't heard me complaining."

"What?" Chantelle squeaked with disdain. "I hug you enough to know what's up, bub. If you're referring to your midsection's teeny-weeny bonus portions of side meat as 'love handles,' you're fired."

Dennis shrugged. "Fire me all you want, sweetheart, but being skinny-fat is a thing."

"Whatever. You're neither skinny nor fat. You're pretty narrow, yet…" Chantelle gestured with her hands, moving them in and out as if doing a sloppy job of playing an invisible accordion. "Comfy."

"Yeah? Huh. 'Preciate it, but when's the last time you saw a shiny and shirtless guy on a magazine cover and thought, 'Oh, wow, how comfy looking'?"

Chantelle tried to recall the last time she'd seen a shirtless guy on a magazine cover at all, but Dennis briefly held his arms out on either side of him before she could think of one. "Nobody wants to see this shirtless," he said, "but I'm not bothered. A supplementary pound of fat here or there doesn't hurt much."

"You don't know how much it hurts until you have to look good in my clothes."

"You'd look good in a knotty oak barrel and saggy rubber galoshes. So if you're gonna make me jog around the world with you and lose my only pair of love handles, it better be for a better reason than the sake of your clothes." Dennis pointed at her book a third time. "Now come on, 'Telle. Don't make me ask again. Be a pal. Chop-chop."

The screech of a train of thoughts coming to a halt on train tracks resounded through Chantelle's brain. An oak barrel and rubber galoshes, huh? Did Dennis just come the closest he ever had to calling Chantelle pretty? She wanted to ask for clarification, but it wouldn't be a good look if he thought she was fishing for compliments, and it was clear he'd already moved on, returning his nosey nose to the fact that she had a book on the table.

Chantelle picked at a corner of the book cover with one finger. "Not hard to tell what this is."

Dennis nodded. "A journal, of course. Or a planner. Or something else most folks just use their phones for nowadays."

"Right the first time." Chantelle walked her fingers over to fiddle with her pen. "I'm sure you can imagine what I'd be doing with a journal."

"You? Sure, I can imagine. A, you're journaling your innermost thoughts and feelings, or B, you're plotting a worldwide overthrow and takeover. If it's B," Dennis said, pointing at himself with both of his thumbs, "I got dibs on being your vice president. Or vice emperor—whatever form of government you're going with."

Although she didn't laugh, Chantelle allowed herself a warm and amused smile. Then she allowed an admission. "Journaling, Jawbone."

"Oh, awesome. Journaling passed by my mind on the way here." Dennis rubbed his hands together and held them open. "Let me see."

Chantelle's face slanted a degree downward, her eyebrow going up. "You're not serious."

"Maybe not." Dennis's hands remained open. "But I'm not playing either."

Chantelle watched his eyes and waited. No, he wasn't playing. He wanted in, and this would be far from the first time she'd ever confided something to him. She took in a breath and removed her phone from the cover of her journal. "Okay. You can see the last page and the last page only."

"The last page? What, you mean the one in the very back that I'll bet is still blank?"

"No, the last page I wrote on." Chantelle opened her journal, flipped the pages, and slid the book across the table.

Dennis's brows crumpled at first, likely on account of his realizing he'd only be getting three words to read out of this deal, but genuine curiosity was in his voice when he read the words aloud. "'Don't pine. Shine.'" He slid the book back over to Chantelle. "Interesting. Feel free to elaborate."

Chantelle closed her journal and took another glance around the restaurant, keeping her voice low. "Well. You remember not too long ago, when my parents had a divorce scare?"

Dennis's eyes popped wide. "Yeah. And they decided to stay together." His head moved slowly up and down before he asked, "They're still all right, aren't they?"

"Oh, yes. They're doing great now. Sometimes so great, it's sickening." Chantelle got a small smile from Dennis by making a gagging face, and she sobered up and went on. "But I've been thinking about their rough patch, how much pain they went through during their communication breakdown. It was like they were sitting on opposite sides of a divide, still in love with each other but not knowing how to get that love over the chasm. So they basically felt unloved while each of them was waiting for the other to fix it somehow."

Chantelle absently placed her phone back on top of her journal. "Plus, the wedding's had me thinking about Alexis and Arthur's rough patch, if you can call it that—when Arthur was with somebody else. Not that I think Alexis was waiting for Arthur, so much, while she went on living her life without him. But I know it wasn't exactly easy for her while she was staying away from him, and *I* was waiting and hoping for him to come around, even if she wasn't. She has more love to give him than any other woman would, but for a while, that love had no place to go."

Having started to tap her pen on her phone, Chantelle caught what she was doing to the screen and stopped herself. "My examples don't quite get at what I'm getting at, but it's a common scenario I've been thinking about, how hard it can be to carry something when you have no one to share it with, or you don't know how to share it. I do see people waiting, in a sense, including friends who post online about their every dating woe and no-go or no-nothing. People waiting to be loved. It can be painful and dissatisfying and—well.

"The thing is, I figure if folks could spend less time just waiting for love and more time finding ways to *give* love, it would help. Not that I think people should try to substitute one kind of love for another, as if having one kind will make their other desires go away. I also don't think people should stay trapped in situations where they're giving and giving to someone while the other person is sitting back, taking and taking. That's not the kind of 'giving love' I mean.

"But it's about finding positive purpose for your heart, not letting life pass by while you're waiting for someone to come along and be or do something for you. It's about discovering what you can be and do for other people, even if it's not in a romantic sense."

"It's about shining instead of pining," Dennis offered, and Chantelle sighed with relief at his understanding.

"Yeah, that," she replied, fingering the corner of her journal again. "I guess I'm not saying it like I wrote it." Falling silent, she looked down at Dennis's hands, which were still sitting open, and then she looked up into his eyes, which were just as open. Open for her to share more with him if she wanted to.

Without further hesitation, she decided. Yes. She wanted to.

Chantelle moved her phone out of the way and reopened her journal to her long, latest entry, flipping past the parts that had Dennis's name in them, and when she determined she had a safe, Dennis-free portion to share, she slid the journal back across the table.

Dennis's look was all business as he read the additional pages, eventually getting back to the three words she'd let him read first, and he peered up at her, his forehead scrunched again but with nothing dramatic about it. "Chantelle," he said. "This is good."

She gave a short, self-conscious laugh. "It's a journal. It isn't supposed to be 'good.'"

"So you forgot that fast who you're talking to?" Dennis drummed his fingertips over the last line he'd read. "You know my blog started out with stuff I first wrote down just for myself."

"I know." Chantelle nodded as Dennis closed her book and slid it back to her. "I guess part of why it isn't 'good' to me yet is that I haven't figured out what I'm going to do about it. How I'm going to shine more, so to speak. I think the message might be right for people who are sitting and waiting, though, you know? It may even be right for Tricia." Chantelle's eyes rolled at her mention of her younger sister, Patricia, who was currently away at college.

Dennis sucked a sharp stream of air through his teeth. "Ouch. Another no-good left her hangin'?"

Chantelle somehow managed to nod and shake her head simultaneously. "I keep trying to tell that girl to stop treating social media like her diary, broadcasting her business to everybody, but yes, she's had another disappointment with another no-good. I wish even more that she'd quit dating for a while and focus on school, since I don't think she's doing the best job of handling both right now. But aside from me feeling some kinda way about these guys I've never met who keep hurting my sister, and also aside from my annoyance that she keeps attracting no-goods in the first place because she's pining and whining instead of growing—"

After cutting herself off with a chortle that instantly cooled the hotness that had begun to rise under her collar, Chantelle confessed, "I guess we all pine and whine and wait around at some point when there're other ways we could be spending our time and emotion. Better ways. It can be easy to lose sight of that, especially if other people around us are pining too. So if we can stop the wallowing, get up, and find a place to shine…" She ended her reflections with a shrug.

"That makes sense," Dennis told her when she didn't go on, and he indicated her book with a nod. "I still say it's good."

Chantelle's lips toyed with a smile. "You ought to know? 'Cause you're the master at journaling and jawing?"

"You know I mean it." Dennis took off his jacket, setting it down beside him on his seat. "I'm not saying you have to copy my tremendous idea and start a blog or something from your scribbles—"

"Thanks for that."

"—but it does make a difference when I share what I have to say. Never thought I'd be into this sort of thing, and now I may be looking at blogging on a full-time basis, soon."

Dennis's voice fell on the end of his sentence, making Chantelle's ears perk up, and when she motioned for him to continue, he continued. "It's not only that I'm sharing what I have to say, but my site gives more people a voice, you know? The discussions that break out in the comments are the best parts, hearing from strangers who read my stuff and speak up, especially folks around our age. I like that we're pushing back against the misconception that it's the norm for younger adults in America now to be entitled slack-offs, loafing around in our parents' basements.

"Not to dismiss how a changed economy plays into the makeup of households these days. And not to ignore that much of what's considered the 'ideal' set and ages of household members is based on culture and conditioned expectations, I'd say, not on concrete natural laws or universal standards. Households look different depending on where you are. But anyway, constantly talking down on a whole generation or two for being lazy and unproductive is unconstructive, not to mention inaccurate. And, well, you read my blog. You know who I think catches a lot of that criticism."

Chantelle sat watching him go at it. He or she or something had switched Dennis's "ON" switch on, and Chantelle was used to buckling up and going along for these rides. She rather enjoyed it. "Creatives," she answered.

"Creatives," Dennis confirmed. "The criticism isn't exclusive to our generation either. Creatives and artists are lazy or impractical or whatever, and their contributions to society aren't all that useful or real compared to other work, right? If that's the case, I'd like us to stop and imagine a world without any movies, old or new, to see or talk about, and no TV shows to watch, except maybe the news. What if there wasn't any fiction or even picture books to read, no comics, no art museums or paintings or sculptures anywhere, no plays or symphonies or ballets to go to? No poetry to recite, no music for dancing or just to listen to, no songs to sing, because no one ever did the work of writing or composing. No novelists, no actors, no playwrights, no animators, no musicians, no comedians, no stage or screen performers anywhere. What kind of society would that be? Would it fulfill us?"

When Dennis paused, Chantelle took the chance to slip her own question in, with a smile made up of something deeper than amusement. "Striking your own nerve by yakety-yakkin', hm?"

Dennis stared at her and eventually said, "Wheels turning." His finger came up to tap at his temple. "About twenty-five percent your fault." He mirrored her smile for a second as he lowered his hand. "You know my audience has been growing while I yak—talk...while I put this kind of stuff out there and all the rest that I write about. And, um, there's something I wanted to tell you." He came to another short pause and took in a breath before asking, "You've heard of Clare Fire Publishing?"

Chantelle blinked a few times at this unexpected turn in the conversation. "Yeah. Can't say I know exactly which books they publish, but I know their name."

"Ah." Dennis used a fingertip to push up his glasses. "Well, I was contacted by one of their editors last week. He's been following *Lawson Jaws*, asked if I've written or if I've considered writing any books, and he says Clare Fire would be interested in working with me."

Chantelle's mouth fell open by degrees. "Dennis." Her stomach gave a surprised jump. "You're getting a book deal?"

Dennis pressed his palms flat on the table, as if he were getting ready to push himself up to his feet. "It would be a book deal, yes. If I send the editor something that'll work. So it could mean it'll be time to leave my automotive job and go full gung-ho into my writing, *Lawson Jaws* and whatever else, for whatever length of time. Striking while the iron is hot."

Chantelle gasped. "White hot!" She partially covered her mouth, making a halfhearted effort to moderate her volume. "Dennis, this is huge! Does anyone else know? Have you told Arthur?"

A grin began to make its way over Dennis's face. "You're officially the first person I've told. Since, you know, our main sidekicks had a big broom-jump coming up in a few days and had enough to think about." He held up a cautioning hand. "But it's not that huge yet. Nothing's set in stone, and getting a book published would mean I'd have to, you know—write one."

Chantelle grinned back at him. "Or you'll do like celebrities and bigwigs do. Hire a ghostwriter."

Dennis's face went immediately deadpan. His upraised hand dropped. "Somebody else's writing, with my priceless name on it?" He gave a snort of superiority. "Not with *this* Dennis, they won't."

"No? Who says the book will say 'Dennis' on it? Maybe despite people knowing you for your blog, Clare Fire will make you write under a nom de plume." Chantelle began scrawling autographs in the air with a decided flourish. "'D.L. Jawson.' 'Noah It All.' 'Seymour Smarty-Britches.'"

"No deal." Dennis swiped a flat set of fingers past his neck. "It's 'Dennis Lawson' or nada. All of me or none of me."

"All of you? Every ounce and morsel, including the side meat you wish could be honest-to-goodness love handles?" Chantelle then sidled past her teasing with a shake of her head. "I'm no expert on how the business works, but I imagine most writers out there aren't being chased down by professionals from places like Clare Fire for possible publication, instead of it being the other way around." She reached a hand across the table, prompting Dennis to do likewise, and he met her in the middle. "Whether a book deal comes out of this or not, I'm already proud of you," she told him, squeezing his fingers.

A sparkle came to Dennis's eyes, his lips slowly curving up on one side. "You're proud of me?" he practically whispered, and he smoothed his hand around until he had a hold of Chantelle's fingers instead. "I'm the one trying to be like you when I grow up. Been trying to keep up with you since college."

Chantelle laughed. "Um, I'm pretty sure I hear an exaggeration somewhere in there, but I'll leave it alone."

Dennis sort of laughed with her but didn't quite. His smile stayed where it was but not quite, perhaps passing into his gaze as it remained locked with Chantelle's.

Out of nowhere, Chantelle became aware of the funny rhythm of her breathing. Wait—was she breathing?

Dennis cleared his throat. "Uh…" He bounced his and Chantelle's clasped hands up and down. "So, yeah. Didn't we meet here to stuff our faces?"

"We did." Chantelle's voice nearly cracked, and she swallowed. "Maybe you should cut out the yakety-yak so we can get to face-stuffing. I waited long enough for your slow self to get here. Did you make a stop around Japan or someplace on your way from the airport?"

"Nope, but maybe I should've gone somewhere else and stayed there for safety. I'm pretty scared to stuff faces with you now." Dennis gave their hands another bounce. "You might try to make me jog off my skinny-fat afterwards."

"Oh, no. I'll let you rest this time." Chantelle slipped her fingers out of Dennis's grasp and pointed upward. "Lord's Day."

Dennis put a hand to his chest. "*Whew.* Thank Him for mercy. Should I pray His mercy endures on Auxiliary Day too, or are you not letting me off the hook for anything that day, regardless? Would buttering you up do any good?" He started to scoot out of the booth. "One warm pat of butter coming up, in the form of service. You sit and relax, and I'll go up and order for both of us."

Once he was on his feet and was about to walk past her to go up to the sandwich shop counter, Chantelle scooted over on her seat as well, but rather than getting up, she reached to stop Dennis with a hand on his forearm. "You think you know what I like?" she quietly asked when he looked down at her, and although she meant to ask it with a challenging smile, as soon as the words were out of her mouth, she wasn't sure if a smile made it through with her question or not.

Dennis didn't smile back at her, if that was any indication of anything. He leaned down toward her, so that she had to tip her head back to maintain eye contact with him. "If it turns out that I don't," he murmured, a strange undertone having crept into his voice, "you'll be more than welcome to set me straight."

Chantelle's scalp tingled. She let go of Dennis's arm. She could formulate no reply.

It was then that he smiled at her, saying, "Here goes nothing," and he turned to continue on through the other lunchers' tables and over to the restaurant counter.

Chantelle watched him go. *"Here goes nothing."* She released a sigh, sitting back and glancing over at her closed journal on the table. *Or everything, I wish.*

Chapter Four

No, Dennis didn't dump everything on Arthur at once after the groom got back from his honeymoon, somehow looking like a billion and a half bucks. Dennis's announcement about Clare Fire was the first piece of news he shared with Arthur, filling Alexis in too, but there was more Dennis kept to himself for a few extra days.

He then took a trip to the Simmons family's firm after the close of a workday, timing his arrival so that he'd get there after Chantelle was sure to be gone but Arthur would still be there, burning a little extended oil to make up for the office time he'd missed while he'd been busy with his new spouse.

Dennis made no ceremony about walking into the building and going to poke his head in the door of Arthur's office, receiving a wave of admittance from the young man who'd been Dennis's main sidekick since even before high school, as the two of them met each other back in middle school. It wasn't the most regular thing for Dennis to come see Arthur here, but this wasn't the first occasion, and Dennis wanted to snag some time between Arthur's work mode and home mode, as Arthur now had someone to go home to and would no doubt be eager to get there soon.

A whole entire wife, *though. Man.*

Crazy to think about, no matter how long Dennis had been friends with the now married couple.

Arthur was sitting at his computer and talking on the phone as Dennis walked over to the desk, so the young men skipped greeting each other verbally, using their free hands to slap palms and bump fists before Dennis set a full bag of cheddary popcorn crisps on the desk, pulled up a chair across from his friend, and pulled out the laptop he'd brought along, also setting it on the desk. The two men didn't say anything once Arthur got off the phone, each of them absorbed in different matters of business, passing the bag of popcorn crisps back and forth between them and crunching away at their snack as they worked, much as had been the custom among their group of friends during daily breaks back in their high school commons.

Neither of them spoke until after Arthur leaned back in his chair and stretched, grabbed two bottles of flavored water from under his desk, and handed one bottle to Dennis.

"Thanks." Dennis accepted the water a handful of seconds before he actually looked up from the screen of his laptop, seeing Arthur run one hand over his brown face and loosen his necktie.

"Dress shirts and ties," Dennis remarked. "You know, I hear tech companies around here are going more casual these days."

Arthur took a swig of his water and shrugged. "Around here isn't *in* here, sir. Not as long as my dad and uncle are still running this place. Besides, I like dressing for work. Wouldn't feel ready to do damage if I rolled up here in a bathrobe and fuzzy slippers."

"*Whoo*. Doing damage. Strong words from a tech-head." Dennis downed a gulp of his own fizzy, citrusy water and dithered over whether to stall with the topic of attire any longer, and then he plunged into his real objective. "So anyway, Arthur, I'm not here to take up all your time. I know you have to get home"—a brief grin flashed over Arthur's face before Dennis finished—"but I think something's up with me and Chantelle."

Arthur rocked back and forth in his chair a few times before he sat up, his face unsurprised. "Oh, you think?"

Dennis froze, staring at his friend. Sarcasm? Over this? From dignified and nerdy Arthur Simmons?

Arthur smiled, shaking his head. "You've been the expert giving me advice on women while you've been stuck in a holding pattern with Miss Chantelle. How long has it been now?"

Dennis's eyes had grown large. "Wait—what? I don't know." He set his bottle of water down on the desk. "How did you...? When—?"

"Alexis first said something about it to me a while ago. Months back. But I saw there was something..." Arthur searched for the words with the rotating wave of one of his hands. "Something different there, when you and Chantelle got back from college. It's still there, but I guess you two have been dancing in circles around it." He lifted his water, raising his eyebrows. "Even when it means you have to take off her heels and give her a foot massage first."

"What?" Dennis's shoulders came up, his hands lifting with astonishment. "I didn't give her a…" Trailing off when Arthur's eye glinted at him, Dennis dropped his hands. "Hardy har. You were supposed to be all into the bride at your reception, not peeking around at what the rest of the wedding party was doing."

"Dennis, it's not like you two were behind a brick wall or something. The whole room saw you. You and Chantelle may be the only ones having trouble seeing it. Or doing something about it, if you do see it."

Dennis slowly closed his laptop. "Huh. Well. Can't say I haven't thought about it," he mumbled, and then he raised his voice to say, "But, come on. I have a way of aggravating Chantelle, and she can get any guy she wants. She has, I guess, but no one's been good enough for her. At least that's how it looks." He started drumming his fingertips on his laptop but quickly cut it out. "It might be corny, but I'm not raring to be the next dude who apparently fails with her."

Arthur drank more of his water and asked, as if he needed to ask, "You've never failed with anybody before?"

Dennis grunted. "Aw, man, you know I have. Who hasn't? It'd be different this time, though." He almost shrugged but couldn't manage it, his voice sinking back to a mumble. "It's Chantelle."

"Hm. Yeah." Arthur did some more rocking in his chair. "So I could give you a lecture about being scared to try, but wouldn't that give you déjà vu, with something reversed?" He drew a flat circle in the air between himself and Dennis, and Dennis gave a single nod of admission, but when he offered no further reply, Arthur said, "All right, so we know she knows how to get a date, but does that tell the whole story? I mean, look at you. You've been out with just as many girls. Maybe more. What do you think that looks like?"

Dennis's eyebrows came closer together. "Point taken." He sat back in his chair, shaking his head. "But, you know, it felt good back in the day. No one in our group was cool in school, but when I could be a guy in goggles and wear high waters to dances and still get girls to go out with me? Yeah."

He reached up to thoughtfully scratch at his cheek. "So I kept it up in college. Pretty much everything except the high waters," he clarified with a short snicker. "The thing is, I've basically been told on a weird number of dates that I'm fun to go places with. Fun. Like an activity partner. A buddy. Big Mr. Fun and Games." Dennis flung a handful of nonexistent confetti into the air. "Now I haven't even been out with anybody that way since…I don't know. Maybe since last year sometime? It started fizzling out after I came back home, I think."

Arthur finished off his water and crushed the empty bottle. "Yup. After you came back home and started fizzling up with Chantelle."

Dennis schooled his features into a straight face, flattening his voice. "That sounds like some mess I would say."

With a shrug, Arthur raised his crushed bottle as if he were going to make an attempt at shooting it over into a nearby bin, but then he simply tossed the bottle onto his desk, a safer bet for him. "You rub off on people, sir."

"Mm." Dennis sat forward, resting his elbows on his knees. "The funny thing about that is, even before the, uh, fizzle-out, no matter who I went out with, Chantelle was the one I kept coming back to. The woman I talked to the most." He rubbed his palms together, heaving a measured sigh. "So, um, I ought to just go for it, huh?"

Arthur put his computer to sleep. "Sure, why not? That is, you can always find reasons why not, if you keep looking for them." He stretched again. "I'm not claiming that I'm the expert or guru or whatever now..." Swiveling to his right as he prolonged his stretch, he brought his left fist conspicuously into Dennis's view.

A groom making a show of his wedding band. That brought a chuckle from his best man.

"...but I say," Arthur went on, "if you know what Chantelle means to you, and I think you do, then show her. Just, however you go about it, I'd suggest you go with something that's more than"—his wedding-banded hand flung a handful of air into the air, possibly meaning to throw confetti, if he'd understood Dennis's previous gesture—"fun."

Dennis remained there for a moment, his head moving up and down while he chewed on his sidekick's suggestion. "Right…" He then sat up, reaching for his laptop as he rose from his seat. "Thanks, man," he said, extending his free hand to Arthur for another fist bump before stopping to dig one more popcorn crisp out of the open bag.

Leaving the rest of the bag for Arthur, Dennis stuck the crisp in his mouth and spoke a direct order around it as he grabbed up his bottle of water and backed away from the desk. "Now *go home*, guru."

Arthur laughed, already getting to his feet.

Chapter Five

The speed with which Dennis figured out a course of action took him by surprise. His entire being received a jolt when the idea first rammed into him, and from that moment on, he took barely a second to second-guess himself about it. He started working on his idea right away, doing a little research and writing out a preliminary sketch, and then he engaged in necessary back and forth over some emails and a video chat.

Once all systems were as "go" as he could get them to be, he made ready to bring the topic up to Chantelle. He waited for an early evening while the two of them were out jogging after work, the lengthening days of spring making time at this time of day for this kind of physical affliction only Chantelle could wheedle Dennis into.

What with the decent amount of other joggers, walkers, and bicyclists out taking advantage of the weather and daylight, Dennis was doing his best not to appear as though he were huffing and struggling his way alongside the lively Chantelle, but he was starting to huff and struggle regardless. This was the same lakeside path they'd done laps on for that charity run in the past. Was Chantelle sure they hadn't jogged a whole bunch of kilometers or millions of miles again today?

"*Gah!*" Dennis eventually belted out with as much vigor as his fatigue allowed him to belt, which wasn't much.

Chantelle glanced over at him, keeping up her pace. "Are you really that tired and out of shape, or just mad? I know you'd rather be bowling right now, or streaming one of those wildlife documentaries you love so much."

"Psh. B-bowling and l-learning about nature," Dennis answered between huffs, "are valuable uses of time. They beat going out shopping for d-dozens of heels that kill your feet and watching drool-worthy rom-coms."

"You mean 'swoon-worthy,' but if you know they're nicknamed 'rom-coms' in the first place, you're more into them than you'll admit. No complaining the next time we watch one."

"Everybody knows those c-cornball nicknames. Rom-coms. Chicken flicks."

"*Chick* flicks, dude. You're being a pain on purpose. And no complaining about 'em."

"If that means the next time we go b-bowling, you won't complain because I don't let you request gutter guards for your r-rampant gutter balling, you've got a deal."

Chantelle laughed at that.

Man. This chick had the strength to toss her head and laugh while running millions of miles.

Dennis's protesting legs and lungs kept up with his jogging companion for a few more minutes before he cried out again. "All right—mercy! Uncle! Wh-whatever the magic word is to stop this dang train. Let me off."

Chantelle sighed. "Fine. We'll stop and rest once we make it back to the spot."

"The spot" was a knoll located beside what could be called the beginning of the path, and Dennis collapsed onto the grass once he and Chantelle reached it. She sat calmly beside him while he leaned back on his elbow, one hand clutching at the stitch in his side.

"My skinny-fat!" Dennis wailed out his agony. If he couldn't successfully hide his exhaustion from the joggers, walkers, and bicyclists around, he might as well go all out in the other direction. His glasses-less eyes clamped to a hard close, his body rolling from side to side as much as it could while he balanced on his elbow. "Oh, my skinny-fat!"

A tapping sensation came to Dennis's knee—a tapping that could otherwise be interpreted as a whacking. "Shut it," Chantelle hissed beside him, and he sensed her looking around. "You're embarrassing me."

Dennis lowered his wail to a whisper that would still be loud enough for his purposes. *"Eli, Eli, lama sabachthani?"* He then popped one eye open to the heavens while keeping the other eyelid tightly clamped, his voice ditching the whisper. "Thy maidservant in Thy manservant's midst calleth this man a pain, and yet hath she no care for the pains in my skinny-fat? Wilt *Thou* hearest me even if it be on this Auxiliary Day? Is not Auxiliary Day also Thine?"

Chantelle leaned over and looked down into Dennis's open eye, a smirk coming to her face. "Keep it up, baby boy, and I'll go get your binky from the car and make you use it out here in front of our Lord and all these people to boot."

Dennis popped his other eye open. He sat up, bumping shoulders with Chantelle as he did so. "If the goal is to get me to shut it, switch the binky to a sucker, and you've got a deal. Cherry or blue raspberry, thanks."

Chantelle's eyes lit up. "You've got suckers in the car?" She then turned off the light. "Wait. We're exercising and being fit today. No candy, no deal. Just put a gym sock in it."

"Like the ones we're wearing now? Sounds gross." Dennis rubbed at his gradually easing stitch, his attitude beginning to sober up. "And there's plenty of a deal, if you want it."

Chantelle reached to snatch a bottle of water from the waist pack she had on. "What do you mean?" she asked, holding back her head to squirt a stream of water into her mouth before she handed the bottle to Dennis.

He accepted the bottle, took in a refreshing stream of water for himself, and watched Chantelle smooth her hair and fuss at the puff she'd gathered it into near the top of her head. She was probably more comfortable with him than she would be with another guy right now, but Dennis knew she'd be a little self-conscious at a time like this, while they were in damp jogging clothes, her hair wasn't at its neatest, and neither of them exactly smelled like a whole bed of roses.

He doubted Chantelle was aware of what it was like for him to see her sun-toasted skin all glistened up this way (his brain self-correcting away from the term "sweaty," as if to avoid offending her on that point, even in his mind) while her person was giving off the inviting scent of cocoa-butteriness mixed with energy and outside and realness.

Dennis's hands gripped tighter at the water bottle. He felt as ready to touch and hold Chantelle now as he'd been at the wedding reception, when she'd been so fancy and floral, settling into his arms and following his lead, trusting him even while her feet were shoeless on the dance floor.

"I mean I did something." Those words from Dennis were almost abrupt as he made the effort to get a hold of his focus, and when he was sure he had Chantelle's attention, he proceeded.

Proceeded to tell her what he'd been working on lately: his emails and video chat with the Clare Fire editor who'd scouted him out, all of it concerning the plans Dennis had come up with for a manuscript…

…and his idea to bring in a co-author for it, because he knew a woman with material that would be perfect for the book's overall message.

The look on Chantelle's face, whatever it was, had gone utterly still.

Dennis didn't stop to try and interpret her look, as he didn't want to lose momentum. "I know that numbers are your specialty," he allowed, "and you probably don't consider yourself to be a writer. I didn't consider myself to be one either before I started blogging. That is, I still don't always think of myself as a writer, but if a writer is someone who has something to say and writes it, then, hey." He shrugged. "I am what I am, and I've been getting what I have to say out there. You could too. You're brilliant, and this could work. Here."

Dennis set aside the water bottle and took one of Chantelle's hands, turning her palm upward and beginning to sketch out an invisible outline on her palm and fingers, explaining a motivational theme inspired by the concept of "shining, not pining." The book would be targeted at an audience of socially conscious as well as socially curious and questioning new adults.

"We wouldn't actually have to say it that way overall," Dennis went on, "about pining and shining. The wording might sound girly. But we can still have it in there because, well, you'd be the author too, and you're a girl."

Chantelle's brow wrinkled, likely on account of the grand revelation at the end of Dennis's sentence.

"I mean, you know you're a girl," Dennis faltered and recovered. "I'm just saying having dual perspectives from male and female co-authors would broaden the scope for the book. We'll talk about how younger adults aren't throwaways, useless, or failures compared to generations before us. We'll describe what younger adults are doing well, how we're contributing to society, what we're up against, and the message will also be a call to action, a call to draw on our collective potential to grow and do more."

Chantelle was chewing on the inside of her cheek, and she appeared to be breathing harder now than she had been during their jog.

"Even a call to the Tricias out there," Dennis added, giving his head a conspiratorial tip toward Chantelle. "Folks may let their older siblings' advice and beef and nagging go in one ear and out the other, but Tricia will have to listen to her sister's advice if it's in the hot new book that everybody's reading, right?" He took a nervous chance at a fleeting, half-teasing smile. "Anyway, since you mentioned having to figure out what you're going to do about what you've been thinking, I thought that saying what you have to say and getting it published could be a part of your own process. Something *you* can do to shine. It'd fit with what I'm doing."

As Dennis finished up, he searched Chantelle's stare, having no time to get lost there while he was busy looking for evidence that his proposal either pleased or displeased her. Or that it shocked her. Or something.

Her eyes fell to her open palm, perhaps reading over the invisible outline Dennis had drawn, and she looked back up at him, the tip of her tongue peeking out to wet her lips. Dennis wondered if Chantelle's throat had parched up at his news, and he was about to pick up her bottle to pass back to her when a shaky murmur made its way from her mouth.

"You'd really want to…write a book with me?"

Dennis's attention slipped down to her hand, where her fingers were moving slightly up and down in a rolling wave, as if waiting to feel his answer.

He answered, meeting her eyes. "I took a gamble. I know my blog is popular, but that doesn't necessarily mean I've got the clout to be calling the shots with a company that's bigger than me, in a market I haven't broken into." Dennis covered Chantelle's open palm with his. "But the thing is, I told Clare Fire that if the woman I have in mind to team up with me isn't interested, I'll go it alone, but if she's game, the only way I'll do a deal for this book is if she's a part of it. They told me to let them know, and we'll go from there."

Chantelle blinked at him several times, her mouth wandering open.

"You don't have to give me a 'yes' or 'no' right away," Dennis told her then. "You can think about it a little while, and we'll talk." He shifted his hand, linking his fingers through hers. "Then if you want to, we'll make a collaboration plan, get some chapters together, and we'll both talk to Clare Fire."

Chantelle's mouth moved around in heavy silence for a few seconds before she managed to say, "Dennis. I don't know what to say."

Warmth spread through Dennis's chest, his eyes making a brief perusal of Chantelle's temporarily underemployed lips, and he raised his gaze with a quiet question. "Her Yakety-Yakness is speechless?"

A small gust of air that could have been a laugh or a sigh burst from Chantelle. After flicking a glance in the direction of passing joggers, walkers, and bicyclists out on the path, Chantelle hid her face, turning in toward Dennis until she was facing behind him, her cheek coming to rest on his shoulder. "You yak as much as I do, Jawbone."

Now sitting there with his own face practically full of the puff of hair on Chantelle's head, Dennis replied with a chuckle, "I beg to differ, Telephone."

Chantelle tucked in closer to him, apparently not caring about their damp jogging clothes and all, and Dennis wasn't bothered either, though he was careful to keep his underarm shut while Chantelle was seeking refuge on his shoulder.

No, he wasn't bothered that this was a rather affectionate display for the two of them in public and that passersby might wonder if the woman at his side was crying (wait—*was* Chantelle crying? He was sensing strong emotion from her, yes, but he didn't hear or feel any crying) and that he had to live with a big hair puff in his face for the time being, unless he turned his head away.

Dennis rubbed his thumb over Chantelle's, relishing this first time he'd ever interlocked fingers with her in this way.

No, he wasn't bothered at all.

Chapter Six

Chantelle could hardly understand the reaction she'd had when Dennis had explained his plans for the book to her. She'd been overwhelmed, and not in a bad way.

Still, receiving the news that a respected publisher had sought out her very own Dennis Lawson had been one thing. Hearing that Dennis wanted her to be his co-author for this significant project was something else, and Chantelle had been at a loss for the words a more sophisticated version of herself would have said when Dennis laid it all out to her.

And a braver version of herself might have taken that opportunity to go ahead and kiss the guy for goodness' sake, as it was the most momentous step he'd ever proposed in their relationship, and it was already such a PDA move on her part to curl into his side the way she did, using his shoulder as a pillow for her so many overwhelmed thoughts.

Her so many thoughts, though, didn't mean she had to think about it, so to speak. She was as good with English as became a professional in her world of numbers, but yes, numbers were her specialty; no, she didn't think of herself as a writer, per se; and here Dennis was, taking a risk with the outcome of one of the biggest opportunities of his life by giving Chantelle the option to share it.

He said he would go it alone if she wasn't interested.

She was interested. She didn't take it lightly, and a part of her feared letting Dennis down if she proved to be unsuitable for this task.

Even so, she didn't have to think about it. She hadn't seen this coming, but there was no way she would have turned Dennis down. So, they planned out their collaboration and got the ball rolling with Clare Fire.

It wasn't a huge shock to Chantelle to find out over the next months that book writing was no easy undertaking, not even while partnering in it with a close friend. She hadn't the experience to know, but perhaps writing a book with a close friend made it even harder in some respects. She and Dennis laid the groundwork for their book with research and data collecting as well as some interviews they conducted with church friends, old high school and college classmates, and people they'd met online. Dennis took key nuggets from his blog to incorporate into the work, and it turned out that Chantelle's strength was in bringing greater emotional development to the material, to ensure that their audience would connect with the message on a human level. A heart level.

However, this process, and Dennis in it, could really get Chantelle's goat. Whenever she jotted notes from life in her journal, she could jot whatever the heck she wanted, with no one else to question her or to criticize the way she worded or pointed out this point or that point, or to say whether or not a particular point needed to be pointed out at all. But writing when the judgment of a co-author mattered was an endeavor she wasn't used to.

Having a partner in this was encouraging on some days, frustrating on others. Sometimes she and Dennis flowed in "the zone" together, and other times they debated or even argued about one section or chapter or another. They called on outside help, including through prayer (without any "wilt Thous" or "also Thines" sprinkled in) and also in sit-down conversations at Dennis's place with Arthur and Alexis, their sidekicks offering input while adding disclaimers about not necessarily taking sides with Author A or Author B.

"Or better said, 'Author D' or 'Author C,'" Alexis amended with a laugh.

At the end of this or that day, Chantelle was so glad to be working on something so important with Dennis, such a friend of hers and a swell guy. At the end of that or this day, Chantelle had trouble recalling why she'd ever set out on this grueling course with Dennis, a man who could be such a bigheaded, opinionated pain in the patootie.

Whatever the case at the end of whatever day, this kind of writing was a new kind of exhausting for Chantelle, and she gained a new respect for all the bona fide writers out there. Having her unfinished writing work sitting on her soul added some difficulty to her ability to concentrate on her job at the software firm during the day, and the challenges of her work at the firm made it hard—sometimes effectively impossible—for her to get her heart and mind together for quality writing in the evening.

"No whining. Get to shining," she scolded herself with a chortle on a couple of nights in her apartment while she sat with her laptop, her brain feeling drained as she tried to figure out how to get where she needed to go next for her share in this manuscript. On some occasions, she did indeed feel like she was inwardly whining and had to snap out of it. Yet, there were times when, after she'd given her all on her day job, everything she tried to write in the evening came out wrong, or whatever words she needed in order to get from Point A to Point B wouldn't come to her at all. She would put her laptop away in defeat at those times, not exactly looking forward to the next check-in she'd have with her co-author.

"How have you been doing this, anyway?" Chantelle up and asked Dennis one Saturday evening that summer while the two of them were lounging on opposite ends of her couch, her foot unapologetically intruding on Dennis's end as they munched at the remainder of their movie snacks in front of Chantelle's now quiet television. "I mean, going hard as a career blogger while not becoming a screw-up at your other job? And now even writing a book on top of it?"

Dennis crunched at a pretzel, appearing unfazed by Chantelle's sudden question that had nothing to do with the wildlife documentary or the romantic comedy they'd just watched together. "Well," he began after chewing and swallowing, "in my case, part of it is in what you said. Brakes and tires are an 'other job' for me, not something I have to put myself into on nearly the same level that you put yourself into your work at the firm."

He dropped his voice as if the two of them weren't the only ones in the room. "Don't say anything about this to the driving public, 'cause I don't want them thinking their tires are gonna pop off in the middle of the highway. But for certain stretches on the job, I can pretty much go on automotive autopilot while my mind is actually on my real work, unless there's some sort of new problem at the shop I haven't run into before.

"Anywho, yeah." Dennis ate another pretzel. "Even with autopiloting, sometimes the hours and stress of it does get to be a bit much, which is a big reason why I cut brakes and tires down to part time. After we send our finished manuscript to Clare Fire, I'll be handing in my two weeks' at the maintenance shop. Not just because my real work is 'fun' for me but because it would suffer if I couldn't put the time and focus into it that it needs as it grows. Career bloggers can't afford to let blog activity lag or to let their content go stale. But, of course, you know that."

"I do." Chantelle popped a multigrain cracker into her mouth and thoughtfully chewed. "I guess I'm starting to see how writing takes so...much, if it's something you really *do*. I mean, kudos and respect to folks who constantly write and can actually do it well while holding down a day job, but it makes sense that you're about to go full gung-ho into, um, your real work. I think I'd turn into a terror if I tried to keep up writing and day-jobbing permanently."

Dennis grinned at her. "You already are a terror, woman. Sometimes I don't know if I'm working with an authoress, a tigress, or a dragon." He used his elbow to nudge her foot away from his side of the couch. "We've been arguing over this book so much, I'll be lucky if you don't loathe my guts and kick my butt to the curb after all this."

Chantelle put her foot right back in the one spot it wanted. "You'll be blessed, bucko. Not lucky. Lady Luck can be the ficklest chick on the block, right?" She left her package of crackers in her lap, holding up both of her hands. "No fickleness here, though. Even if I do loathe your guts after this, I won't kick you to the curb. I'll let you stick around, so that I can burn you to a crisp daily for how you've been acting since we got started on the book. It's not like you've been a perfect and angelic genius with all the right answers for everything." She converted her raised hands into make-believe claws and let out a growly roar, breathing fire across the couch.

"Nah. No crisping here." Dennis didn't dodge her fire, his grin lessening without dimming, his voice a murmur. "I can take the heat."

While the particular burst of fire between them went out with a puff of smoke, Dennis's comment did anything but make the room chillier.

Chantelle's insides shivered with warmth as she lowered her hands.

Dennis blinked hard, half-shaking his head. "But is the book stressing you out too much? I know writing for publication comes with a different weight than, like, writing college papers."

"Oh, no, no," Chantelle said with a shake of her own head. "The book's message is timely, so I'd rather we get it done than drag it out. Even if I can't do this long-term, I'm doing it now." She munched on another cracker. "It's kind of like a pregnant lady in labor. She can give birth all right, but she couldn't go through that every day, and some women who go through it only do it once. One and done."

Dennis's expression wavered between amusement and worry. "Are you saying working with me on this is as painful as childbirth?"

"Hm? Oh. Dunno." Chantelle shrugged. "I'll let you know for sure when I'm a pregnant lady in labor." She then nearly bit down on her tongue as her mind displayed a visual of her joke. Was she implying that Dennis would be there with her when she did experience childbirth someday?

Goodness. She had to keep a hold of herself, but it was difficult with Dennis looking at her the way he was now, as he seemed to be doing pretty often lately. Not only was Chantelle aware of a different intensity that had been growing between them over the months, but partnering with

Dennis on so meaningful a project gave her a more intimate sense of his passion for his work.

Yes, Chantelle was honored and grateful that he'd chosen to share this project with her, but it was Dennis who truly loved this endeavor as more than a worthy but grueling task with some bright spots in "the zone." Chantelle wanted the book to be finished, wanted to see it on bookstore shelves one day, while Dennis wanted the same but was also thriving on the writerly grind required to get there.

Chantelle hadn't fully imagined what her actions might lead to, that day at the park when Dennis's undeclared but deepening discouragement over his derailed career plans had weighed so heavily on Chantelle that she'd taken Dennis's head in her hands and reminded him of the mind that was still his. Seeing him make moves with such purpose since then, seeing him build something that made people stand up and take notice made Chantelle admire that mind of his the more.

Now with her getting hands-on experience with his passion, whether she and Dennis were flowing together or arguing with each other or something in between—if Chantelle hadn't previously been certain of what she had in her heart for Dennis Lawson, this whole process with him was leaving her with little doubt on the matter.

It was the biggest factor that might have been making her writing easier or harder. Or both.

At any rate, Chantelle kept at it with Dennis until they completed their manuscript that fall and sent it off to Clare

Fire, and the co-authors fist-bumped and high-fived each other all over the place.

"There'll be work ahead to get the thing fit for public consumption," Dennis reminded Chantelle between high fives. "I hear the editing phase is the part that makes a lot of authors go gray or bald, and then we won't get to see the book in print till next year. But hey, Chantelephone! We've made it this far."

Chantelle's excitement was mixed with relief, and feelings of accomplishment warred with her nerves about the editing that was still ahead, but Dennis was right. They'd made it this far, and he said the milestone called for a real celebration.

"Getting a full night's sleep for the first time in forever," Chantelle suggested. "*That* sounds like a heavenly celebration to me."

"Uh, yeah, no. You think saints and angels in the glorious heavenly realms are wasting time to lie around and go to sleep?" Dennis scoffed. "Come on, we can do better than that. Give me a minute to think about it."

Chantelle gave Dennis a few days to think about it, while she rewarded herself with some full nights of sleep she'd been missing for months.

Dennis then called her up on a Wednesday, telling her to get ready for that Friday night. "I suggest you wear red, or red and black," he said. "Something nice but comfortable enough to move around in. And for the love of eggs and bacon—pick a pair of shoes that won't make your dogs bark. Or, *ahem*, won't make your puppies yip." After snickering over the phone, he slowly added, "Oh, and, um...maybe you can wear a red flower in your hair? Please? Like you did at the wedding."

Chantelle's eyebrows lifted, all kinds of little somethings playing into the smile that tentatively tugged on her lips.

So. Dennis had taken more notice of her at the wedding than she'd thought. That ending request of his had sounded hesitant and rather endearing. Even sweet.

Dear Lord. What is this? By any broad or slim chance in heaven or on earth or in the known universe, could that have been Dennis's way of asking Chantelle...on a date? Kind of a mystery date? Or would this really be no more than a "we finished our manuscript" celebration as friends and authors?

Once the phone call ended minutes later, Chantelle scarcely knew what to do with herself.

Nevertheless, that Friday, she governed herself according to Dennis's suggestions and request, painting her fingernails a fierce crimson shade; dressing in a red, A-line tunic dress with satiny black leggings and shiny red flats; smoothing on red, smudge-proof lip color (in case...something might happen tonight, lip-wise); and fastening a red rose into her billow of hair. A faux rose she could reuse sometime if need be.

But it wasn't a faux rose Dennis had in his hand when Chantelle opened her apartment door to him that evening. The single, long-stemmed red rose Dennis held was a real one, set off against his all-black outfit, the trim lines of his shirt and pants serving as a fine accentuation to his build.

As Chantelle looked him over, no thoughts of skinny-fatness or even pretty-narrow-but-comfiness came to her mind. Just hotness. The hotness of a swaggering geek-at-heart with eyes sparkling behind his glasses.

"You'll want to hold on to that," Dennis told her as he gave her the rose, and when they reached his car in the apartment complex parking lot, he opened Chantelle's door for her first.

Oh, let the saints and angels sing in the glorious heavenly realms above and beyond. This had to be a date.

As a small bouquet of additional roses sat in the backseat of Dennis's car, he mentioned possibly needing to stop by the car to grab one of the extras if the rose in Chantelle's possession "gets dropped or trampled on or something," and the end of their drive through town brought them to a dance hall.

"Tango night," Dennis finally explained after he'd come around to open Chantelle's door, and she all but leapt out of the car with enthusiasm and delight, despite the fact that she didn't exactly know how to tango. As far as she knew, neither did Dennis.

It was no matter, though, as the tango night in the dance hall opened with an instructional session, with Dennis and Chantelle and about ten or twelve other couples learning the steps from two ballroom dance instructors. Following the session, the couples were free to party on the dance floor with what they'd learned, and Dennis, with an almost sly smile on his face, whispered to Chantelle, "All right, lady. You know what to do."

He whisked Chantelle past a table where she'd set her rose down during the instructional portion, and she did indeed know what to do, though she had to get some laughing out of the way before she brought the rose to her mouth and held it by the stem between her teeth as she and Dennis continued to dance.

Dip me once, and dip me twice, and dip me once again, my bestest man.

Chantelle did a lot of laughing that night, as did Dennis, both of them taking the tango quite seriously without taking it too seriously, teasing each other for their mistakes and adding a flourish and flare to the energy they put into their moves. As Chantelle basked in the familiarity and newness of dancing in a new way with the companion she'd danced with plenty of times before, she wasn't afraid to admit to herself that she was having, yes, a *fun* night with Dennis. Fun, fiery, playful—and, she dared to think at last, romantic.

After they'd tangoed a fulfilling stretch of the evening away and left the dance hall, they stopped by a parlor for ice cream (that is, Dennis got an ice cream sundae while Chantelle chose a cup of frozen yogurt) before Dennis drove Chantelle back home.

She was holding the bouquet of roses when she unlocked her apartment door and then turned to Dennis, grinning up at him as she pulled her single back out and again held the rose between her teeth.

Dennis gave a warm chuckle. "Mm. So you're going to sleep like that?"

Chantelle chortled and spoke around the rose. "You betcha. All night." She then removed the flower from her mouth and took a step closer to Dennis. "For real though, this was an incredible idea to celebrate, Dennis. I had a great time."

Dennis stared down at her, his eyelids lowering somewhat as he also took a step closer to her, and Chantelle instinctively held her breath, her heart setting off in its own tango of anticipation.

There came a heavy pause, during which Dennis's jaw moved around in what appeared to be some uncertainty, and he exhaled, his face taking on a different light as he pushed out a short laugh, saying, "Well, 'Telle. What did you expect from the master, huh?"

And with that, Chantelle's anticipation sputtered and vanished into nothingness. What was left of her smile sank away, her roses similarly sinking to her sides, the single in one hand and the small bouquet in the other.

Right. Dennis, a non-Romeo but nonetheless the master at this type of thing. The dating thing. If this thing had, in fact, been a date.

Chantelle had been out on enough of her own dates to tell what they were. What made it so hard to tell this time?

"Yeah," she eventually replied, her cheeks heating up, her voice low and now hoarse. "You did make this look easy, didn't you? Even though I wasn't on the outside looking in this time."

Dennis's features went blank for a moment. "What?" he asked, and then his eyes slowly widened, his foot taking what might have been an involuntary step backward as he held his hand up. "Oh, no, Chantelle. That's not what I…"

He trailed off, his uncertainty clearly coming back, and Chantelle hated feeling a comedown before the night was even over, hated the embarrassment that had begun to prickle over her.

While lowering her eyes, she pressed her smudge-proof lip-colored lips together. Might as well keep them from trembling.

Chapter Seven

"Knit one, purl one. Knit one, purl one," Chantelle repeated to herself when her conversation with Alexis reached a pause the next afternoon. Chantelle had come over to visit Alexis at home, and both the young women were sitting with fabric and knitting needles in the living room, Chantelle's needles plodding while her friend's needles were flying.

Chantelle looked up from the chair she was sitting in across from Alexis, who was on the couch. "I've been knitting one and purling one like crazy over here," Chantelle said, "and mine still doesn't look like yours."

Alexis took a quick glance up from her work, a smile coming to her plump, light brown face. "Chanting 'knit one, purl one' out loud as you go along doesn't mean your fingers are actually doing it." Her kinky chestnut curls bounced a bit as she nodded toward Chantelle's fabric. "Or maybe it's because you're doing it like crazy, and your results are the crazy version."

"Ha! Whatever." Chantelle knitted one and purled one. Sort of. "It's true what they say, though. Knitting is relaxing. Even if I'm doing it wrong."

"You're doing fine. Wrong and fine." Alexis laughed. "And you can come over here to relax a little more, you know. You've barely been over since I moved in with Arthur."

Chantelle's smile was vague as her eyes concentrated on her fingers and needles. "Thanks, Lexi, but you're a wife now. No married folks want their friends barging in at their place all the time."

"I didn't say come over all the time. I said 'a little more.' I'm Mrs. Simmons now, yes, but I'm still Alexis. Arthur is still Arthur." Alexis gave a tiny titter. "Don't you and Dennis abandon us just because we broom-jumped, as Dennis would say."

Chantelle's plodding needles came to a stop. "Yeah," she mumbled, dropping her fabric to her lap and her eyes to the floor. She ground one of her slipper-socked feet into the living room carpet. "Dennis."

Alexis's needles didn't stop but did slow down, her gaze moving back to her friend. "Something wrong?"

Chantelle shook her head, tapping her feet together, but when she looked up and saw Alexis waiting for a better answer than that, she decided to come out with it. "You know Dennis and I finished our manuscript." After her friend confirmed that fact with a nod, Chantelle went on. "Well, we went out to celebrate last night. Dennis took me dancing. To learn the tango, of all things." The fun, fiery memory of it made Chantelle pause to take in and release a breath. "It was wonderful. Dennis was wonderful, and even though we hang out all the time, I thought we were on a date last night. An actual date."

Chantelle's eyes began to sting. She hated it. "But when he brought me home, he brushed it off like the night had been a joke to him. Like maybe he went all Romeo on me because it's something he knows how to do." Her nose burned, and the sting in her eyes was turning into dampness. "Like he knows how to turn it on with a woman, whether or not it's personal."

Alexis's needles had come to a full halt, and her work settled in her lap. When Chantelle stopped, Alexis inserted a quiet observation. "You mean, whether or not it's *you*."

Chantelle's shoulder came up and fell. "Maybe. He and I texted real quick this morning to plan to meet for lunch after church tomorrow. I'm scared it'll be weird," she muttered, and when a warm spill slipped through her eyelashes and down to her cheek, she let out a throaty laugh. "Oh, doggone it, why am I crying?" She nearly used the fabric hanging on her needles to dab at her face, but then she thought better of it, gathering a part of the long sleeve of her purple top to do the job.

Once her face was reasonably dry, she said, "I'll bet you already pieced this tidbit together or have at least had some suspicions, but I started liking Dennis while we were away. College. It seemed like he was always out with somebody else, though. I kept on dating too because it was fun and, well, a girl's gotta date sometime if she wants to. Besides, how would it look, me sitting around like nobody wanted me while Dennis was out kickin' it with other girls?" Chantelle fiddled with her needles without knitting one or purling one. "It feels pretty silly when I think about it now, and dating kind of fizzled out for me after Dennis and I got back from college."

That part of her explanation gave her pause. It had indeed been quite a while since Chantelle had been out with a guy that way. Had she, without planning it, put her dating life on hold because she was waiting for Dennis?

With a groaning sigh, Chantelle continued. "In movies and books or whatever, it seems like two people going from friends to more should be the easiest thing in the world." She let go of her knitting and pretended to pull her hair out. "Sometimes I wanna scream at the characters, 'It's not that complicated! Quit lollygagging and drumming up flimsy excuses and just go for it already! Goodness gracious.'"

She dropped her hands with a plop on her lap. "But when it's real life—*your* life, your friend, your relationship on the line, it's not so easy to cross that point of no return, with no guarantees you'll be happy and lovey with him in the end, instead of ending up with a drastically changed and awkward friendship that will either recover from the awkwardness or gradually die because it's too hard to keep it going when some major feelings in the relationship are only one-sided."

Alexis's eyes enlarged at that, a question sliding from her mouth with a teasing kind of seriousness. "Girl, who you tellin'?"

Chantelle nodded vigorously, tossing a wave toward her friend. "Right! Right." It was nice to have someone who understood. "And, hey, this may sound stupid, but I've worried about being, well, about being a copycat. Like maybe becoming more than friends with Dennis seemed like a good idea because things worked out for you and Arthur."

"Oh yeah?" Alexis shook her head. "If that's what you're worried about, it's already too late for you to be a copy of me and Arthur. You haven't been into Dennis this way from the day you first met him. Besides, you're correct." She infused some thickness into her tone for a second. "'Well, uh, maybe I shouldn't be with Dennis because I don't want to be a copycat' does sound stupid. Because it's stupid. You wouldn't have feelings for Dennis for years now and desire another level of relationship with him just because of some impulse to imitate. Toss that in the 'flimsy excuses' bucket and forget it."

Chantelle's face became somewhat warm with sheepishness, but because she was getting needed relief by having a sounding board for her thoughts about this, she went on. "Probably another one to toss, here, but he's not the most romantic guy. Dennis." Her voice dropped a confidential notch. "He calls me 'Chantelephone,' or sometimes just 'Telephone.' It's nice because it's our own dorky little thing, but 'Telephone' isn't the kind of name to go with sweet nothings whispered in a woman's ear." She gave a quivery chortle. "That kind of nickname is fun. Dennis is such a fun guy to me. With me. But the fun can make it hard to tell whether or not I'm special to him, special in a different way than…"

As Chantelle left the verbal side of her thought unfinished, Alexis's head moved faintly up and down. "So," Alexis began, "you and Dennis haven't taken the leap to be more than friends. Not officially, anyway"—if Alexis saw the surprise that came over Chantelle's face at that part, Alexis didn't acknowledge it—"but you're expecting him to be romantic with you? To treat you like you're his girlfriend or something when you're not?"

Chantelle's mouth came open, but when she didn't answer, Alexis moved on with, "Table that, because on the other hand, who says your own dorky little things can't be romantic too? Arthur and I danced to Christmas jams on our wedding day, and it was the most romantic thing for us. And who says Dennis hasn't been romantic with you in general, or that he hasn't made any romantic moves?" She tossed something invisible toward the floor. "Are you waiting for him to throw flowers at your feet daily, or to come to your complex and give you midnight serenades outside while you listen and swoon from your balcony in the moonlight?"

Chantelle sat back in her seat. "No…" was all she managed to get out of her open mouth.

"No?" Alexis held up a cautioning hand. "Now, don't take this the wrong way. You know I love you, I know you're a genius, and you're amazing at what you do," she said before letting her caution lower, her eyes holding firmly to Chantelle's. "But, honey, Clare Fire Publishing never heard of you. You weren't a part of the writing and publishing world they move and print and scout in. They wanted Dennis, the man making waves with *Lawson Jaws*, and that man basically told them no deal, no contract, no book if he couldn't have you as his co-author, unless you didn't want to do it. Dennis can act like a clown sometimes, but he's no idiot, and he took a chance with his own big chance to give you a chance to step up to a new challenge. You think he would've done that for a woman he doesn't admire and respect?"

Chantelle's mouth came to a close.

Both of Alexis's hands went to her chest. "I'm saying this as a woman. I mean, I can't say it as a man anyway." She chuckled at herself and went on. "But sometimes I think women want their prescribed ideas about romance with a man more than they want an actual man. A human man.

"Look at me right now, here with you while my mister is out at the office on a Saturday. You know, he had to put in some extra hours during the week, the first weeks after we got married. No, it's not like that every week, and no, he doesn't go to work every Saturday." She briefly held up an adamant finger. "And trust me, if Arthur ever did get all workaholic on me, he and I would talk, since the two of us only seeing each other during two-week vacations every year isn't the plan.

"But he let me know before the wedding that he'd need to make up some time at the firm after our honeymoon. When he went back to work, I could have sat around thinking how unromantic it was that we were newly married and he wasn't spending twenty-four hours a day all up in my face. Or I could remember, like I do now, that a major reason why he's staying so serious about his work is for me. For our future together. For a home we'd like to buy someday. For any babies that come along."

Alexis then reached for the knitting in her lap to get back to it. "Plus, he's supporting me now so that I can put my all into growing my own business," she said, holding up her work for a second, "and I got to quit my file clerk job—a line of work that's becoming more obsolete anyway as technology advances."

Alexis's needles resumed their flying, knitting and purling. "Being married to a successful businessman will mean he has to put in longer days sometimes, and some six-day workweeks. He'll do his thing while I'm doing my thing, and we'll rejuvenate each other when he gets home." After her exaggerated eye-roll of pleasure drew a small laugh from Chantelle, Alexis said, "It's natural and right to desire to be romanced, to want to feel it, and to be sure it's the real thing. To be sure it isn't a joke, in your case. Still, you know good and well that not everything you've imagined about love and romance is going to play out that way in real life."

Giving Chantelle another direct look, Alexis asked her, "So, what's bigger for you? Your desire for romance or your love for Dennis?"

It would've been impossible to miss the liberty Alexis had taken in naming what was in Chantelle's heart, but Chantelle held no objections to it. "That shouldn't even be a question," she murmured. Then, slowly sitting up in her chair, she admitted, "There's no way I couldn't know that Dennis cares for me and respects me, and I respect and care for him. But what if he still doesn't care for me in the other way, you know? There've been times lately when I thought he might, but overall I'm not sure."

"Hm." Alexis's lips curved upward. "Why don't you take a lesson from your own book, chica? Don't pine. Go to him and shine. Maybe blow his mind." While the weight accompanying her next words was obvious, she didn't give up her smile. "And if he doesn't want that kind of relationship with you, at least you'll know, so you can deal with it instead of wondering."

Chantelle sat chewing on that, inwardly weighing the weight. Was she ready to deal with the reality of Dennis not returning her feelings, if it came to that? She didn't feel ready, but after the fun, fire, and ending weirdness of the night before, she knew that keeping the status of her and Dennis's relationship in limbo would help nothing.

After a sigh, Chantelle picked up her fabric and needles, needing to get back to the relaxation. "Knit one, purl one. Knit one, purl one." Then, with an ironic but light snort of humor at herself, she began to chant, "He loves me, he loves me not. He loves—"

Following a snort of her own, Alexis cut in with, "Oh, knock it off," and the laugh the two women shared lifted some of the weight—if not in Chantelle's heart, at least in the room.

Chapter Eight

"I figure if folks could spend less time just waiting for love and more time finding ways to give *love..."*

Cringe.

"It's about discovering what you can be and do for other people..."

Oops.

"Don't pine. Shine."

Ouch. The good Lord help her.

Chantelle had in no way limited those love-based sentiments of hers to romantic situations. Even so, that didn't mean the sentiments couldn't apply just as well when this particular kind of love was the case, and it was uncomfortable to have her own words coming back to bite her. Even if the biting was for good reasons.

After leaving Alexis's company on Saturday, Chantelle wasted no time in brainstorming her next step. The coming Monday would be a significant day: Dennis would be handing in his two weeks' notice at the auto dealership's maintenance shop. Although Chantelle would've liked to make something of it on that day or on Dennis's actual last day at the shop, Chantelle didn't want to wait that long to make her move, dragging out the "friends or what?" question between her and Dennis. Because they intended to meet for lunch on Sunday, it could be the best opportunity for Chantelle to go for it.

She didn't have any new publishing deals to offer to split with Dennis, nor did she have any tango or salsa or rumba lessons planned, and she wouldn't be bringing Dennis roses to hold in his teeth. Yet, ready or not, she was going to put her own words to work and take a shot at giving something she'd been waiting to receive, in a sense.

Men desired to be romanced and wanted to feel it and be sure it was the real thing too, didn't they?

Chantelle went shopping early Saturday evening and texted Dennis to say she'd want to go home and change after church the next day before meeting him for lunch. She figured that would buy her some extra minutes, but she was still a little late when she pulled up in the sandwich shop parking lot Sunday afternoon. She chose a parking spot that was a ways off from other cars in the lot, and Dennis was out on the curb in front of the shop, waiting, his hands in his jacket pockets.

Chantelle felt a twinge in her middle as she wondered if Dennis had stayed outside instead of going inside to wait in their booth because he was worried she wouldn't show up. He spotted her car and started making his way over while she parked, and when she opened her car door, he smiled with evident relief, holding out his hands and calling to her, "Hey, what did you do? Make a stop around Japan or somewhere on your way from home? Why'd you park all the way over here in the boonies?"

Chantelle ran her hands over the sides of her pea coat after she climbed out of the car, in case her palms were damp, and she shut her door, opened one in the back, and stood there.

When Dennis stopped where he was, his hands dropping and his smile faltering with hesitation, Chantelle beckoned him forward. "It's okay. Over here."

It's okay, she repeated to herself, trying to calm her quaking nerves.

Dennis obeyed her beckoning, and once he was within reach of Chantelle, she took a hold of his open jacket, pulled him nearer to her, gazed up into his eyes until his look thoroughly softened and her nerves quieted, and she commenced to ease Dennis's jacket back and down from his shoulders.

"*Whoa.* Oh. Okay," Dennis murmured with a hint of a question in his voice as Chantelle took the jacket off of him, and he stood there in his casual button-up and jeans while Chantelle stowed his jacket in her car and unzipped a garment bag she had hanging back there.

Chantelle relished the combination of confusion, warmth, and amazement on Dennis's face as she pulled a robe out of her car: a long, burgundy cape of a robe lined with faux fur.

Taking a couple of steps around Dennis, Chantelle draped the robe over his shoulders, and then she came back around to fasten the robe in the front. Next, she pulled a golden crown with a burgundy dome out of her car and reached to settle the crown on Dennis's head, lightly tugging at the fur around the crown's base until it seemed secure enough not to shift around. Then, the last item Chantelle pulled from her car was a golden scepter, stunning in its plastic and shining faux gems, and she handed the scepter to Dennis with a slight curtsy and a dip of her head.

As Chantelle stood back and looked Dennis over, she couldn't help grinning. What instinct this geek-at-heart had. Without even fully knowing what was going on, he was already striking a stately pose, his chest out and shoulders back, his hand holding the scepter to his front with a grand grip.

Chantelle shook her head. "I've got you looking like a whole prom king out here."

Dennis adjusted his feet to enhance the grandness of his stance. "Have I got my months wrong?" Another adjustment to his feet, and a quirk of his eyebrow. "Is it my birthday? Or—ah *ha*!" He pointed his scepter toward her. "You've accomplished your worldwide overthrow and takeover, and I am now vice emperor of the planet. This is it?"

Chantelle simply watched him, smiling more to herself than at him, and then she stepped forward. "Yes, this is almost it, but it's a different 'it.' A rumor is circulating through the land that you, Your Jawness, will be handing in your two weeks' at a certain place of employment tomorrow, so that you'll be free to move into the next phase of your life, jawing heartily all the way."

The playful aspect began to melt away from Dennis's demeanor, and he lowered his scepter to his side as Chantelle came close to him, her voice also losing its playfulness and gaining a thick layer of emotion as she said, "So I wanted to hail your coming change by telling you that I'm proud of you, I'm grateful for you, and…"

Chantelle's next action might have been against protocol, her taking hold of the front of a king's royal robe, but she did it anyway. A marked incandescence came to Dennis's countenance as Chantelle stared up at him. A gleam was slipping into his eyes, and that familiar verve emanating from him made Chantelle positively lightheaded.

Her heart beat to the rhythm of her inevitable intention.

Tell him. Tell him…

She'd tell him, in the most fitting way for this point in time. Their time.

It took only the gentlest pull on Dennis's robe for him to lean, meeting Chantelle in the middle, and she closed her eyes right before her lips touched his and made themselves at home there.

Good gravy. Warm butter. Sweet heavens.

Living Dennis.

Would Chantelle have waited so long to kiss this man if she'd known precisely how it would be to savor him this way? If she'd known how tender and alive his response would be?

After a satisfying slice of forever, Chantelle pulled back, opened her eyes, and nearly hiccupped with surprise.

The heat of their kiss had added steamy spots to Dennis's glasses.

Chantelle gave him a second to reach up and slide his glasses off, and then she cycled back to finish the thought she'd started aloud. "I'm grateful for you, and you mean everything to me."

The heavy breath Dennis let out then was a release for them both. He slipped an arm around her, asking, "So you forgive me for that stupid joke I made the other night?"

Chantelle tipped her head to one side. "Dennis…"

"Because sometimes it's easier to crack a joke," he hurried on. "Especially when I've been trying to show an awesome woman what she means to me, and I know she could have any man she wants, but she's been hanging around with me, of all people."

"You 'of all people'? Oh, Dennis, why would you—?"

"And I'm not the best at saying what I feel when it's so personal. Maybe articulating affection doesn't come easy when it isn't something you came up hearing. Even my parents didn't—couldn't, um, after Myles…"

Chantelle's stomach dropped when Dennis's voice broke.

Little Myles. Dear God.

Dennis's jaw clenched while he got a hold of himself, and then he continued. "But if you were to ask around the world to find out how many people I call my 'Telephone,' there'd only be one. I mean, whether or not I did make it look easy back then, dating or whatever, no matter who else I went out with, you were the woman I'd come back to when I really needed to talk, when I really wanted to listen. I kept ending up with you." The corner of Dennis's lips shuddered upward. "Here you are, still. The numbers geek with the number I dial."

The rhythm of Chantelle's heart could have beat out a number then. "Talking and listening," she mused. If it was possible to feel a light bulb clicking on in one's soul or to feel the glow of morning dawn on one's face in the afternoon, Chantelle felt it. "Dennis. *That's* why you call me that?"

Dennis shrugged and nodded at the same time. "Well, 'Cellphone' would be more accurate, technically, but it doesn't go with ''Telle.' Besides, for folks who still have home phones, they're telephones, and being with you is home for me. I never feel like a guest or a stranger with you. You're just home." His forehead scrunched. "Is that stupid?"

Chantelle let go of the front of Dennis's robe so that she could work her hands upward, her arms making their way around Dennis's neck as she said, "If I tell you, 'Not stupid at all. It's the most romantic thing from a man who's got romance coming out of his ears,' will you acknowledge that you talk and yakety-yak-yak it up as much as I do, Jawbone?"

Dennis's shuddery half-smile lost its shudder as it gave way to a grin with all the light and zest of summertime, regardless of the fall chill in the air around them. "Nope," he replied, his other arm coming around Chantelle, albeit the angle was slightly awkward to prevent his scepter from poking into her back. "Don't wanna be caught lying on the Lord's Day just to please my lady."

"Oh, no. Never that," Chantelle said with a laugh, although hearing Dennis call her his lady made the laugh rather croaky. She had to clear her throat. "In other news, excuse me for my lateness in getting here. Were you worried I might not come? We should've been stuffing our faces by now."

Dennis shook his head. "Aw, we'll get to that in a minute." He leaned in again, whispering, "Somebody's face has more important stuff going on, at the moment."

Chantelle had barely a second to smile about that before Dennis interrupted her smile with a slow kiss, deeper than their first, followed by warm stamps of affection he pressed along her cheek and on the tip of her nose and over to her other cheek.

It took the slamming of a car door somewhere else in the parking lot for Chantelle to come to, not realizing until then how far she'd been lulled into dreaming while awake.

"You…" Her closed eyelids fluttered open. "Dennis? How long were you standing out here before I got here? You must be getting cold."

"So? If I am," Dennis mumbled against her cheek, "it's one hundred fifteen percent your fault." His mouth moved to her ear. "You stole my jacket, woman. My phone too, in the pocket."

"Oh." Chantelle wrinkled her nose, and then another light clicked on for her. "Well, what do you need your phone for anyway? No one else to call." She pulled back again and cheesed at Dennis. "I'm right here."

His eyes narrowed at her. "Don't go misusing my metaphor as a license or excuse to steal my literal property." He inclined his head to settle his cheek against hers. "*Tsk, tsk, tsk.* So fresh out of church, sister, and you're out here robbing and thieving and conniving around."

Chantelle sighed, resting in Dennis's secure hold a moment longer. She then removed her arms from his neck, reluctantly stepping back to end their embrace. "And we're out here PDA-ing. I did park in the boonies, but maybe we've still caused enough of a scene for today."

Dennis put his glasses back on. "If you think this is something—I'm about to scarf down a meatball sandwich in public with a super-king cape on and a big ol' crown on my head."

Chantelle's eyes grew round, and she waved a hand down the length of Dennis. "Oh, no, you don't have to wear this all through lunch." She then fetched Dennis's jacket and her purse out of the car. "You can put your coat back on or whatever."

"Can't back out now, sweetheart. Hand me my cell and put the jacket back in the vehicle." Dennis again held his scepter to his front, his posture erect. "This flashy and magnificent getup is your doing. So I'm going to wear it to the auto shop tomorrow, wear it the next time we go jogging, and I'll have it on when we get our author photos taken, and when we—"

"Oh, help us all," Chantelle mumbled as she dug into a pocket of Dennis's jacket, took out his phone, and tossed the jacket back into her car, giving Dennis's kingly look another look-over. "What have I done?"

Dennis gave the fingers of his free hand a loud snap. "I've got it! This can be the start of our foray into fiction."

"Fiction?" Chantelle shut and locked up her car. "*Our* foray into fiction? Our nonfiction hasn't even been born yet. Not officially, but you're out here talkin' about some foray. Who says—?"

"A novel! Better yet, a screenplay." Dennis pointed and swept his scepter toward the great expanse of the land beyond. "We can go around town together while I find a bunch of guaranteed ways to embarrass you in my getup. Then we'll use the material to co-write a drool-worthy chicken flick."

Forcing out a groan to stifle her urge to laugh her noggin off, Chantelle marched her way over to Dennis, slapping his cellphone to his chest to make him take it in hand as she muttered, "Okay, dude, you're fired," and she proceeded to march past him toward the sandwich shop.

Dennis circled to follow right on her heels, his turn an exaggerated one that made his cape of a robe fly around him as much as possible. "Um, why would you fire a guy who's about to hand in his two weeks'?"

Conceding the futility of her efforts against it, Chantelle gave up and got some hard laughing out of the way in the seconds prior to her walking rather proudly into the sandwich shop on the arm of a majestic and lovable pain in the patootie who apparently didn't yak as much as she did but who, nonetheless, seemed to have no idea how to shut up.

Bonus:
"Catnap in a Coffee Shop"
An Excerpt from another romantic comedy,
The "She" Stands Alone

I should've brought my library book.

So went the last thought I remembered having before I found myself shuddering out of an unwelcome catnap. The side of my face was smashed into my left, propped-up hand while the open newspaper, a partially eaten sandwich, and half a cup of cold coffee sat before me. My eyes took a furtive glance around at the other coffee shop patrons, wanting to be sure I wasn't being watched before I assessed the amount of drool that I felt had passed into my hand while I'd been dozing.

No such luck. One couple had brought a little boy along for breakfast. The boy—who was indeed little but who looked big enough to know better—apparently had no problem with the unrelenting stare he was leveling on me while he nibbled his hash browns.

"Now she's lookin' at me, Mom," he announced before his parents could shush him, and his mother turned to toss a hasty smile of apology at me, clearly eager to squelch the situation.

The boy was duly shushed, his parents distracting him and making an unspoken but conspicuous show of acting like they'd never seen the woman snoozing away over there by the windows. But their son's announcement had managed to catch the attention of other coffee shop guests. I wished they'd all hurry up and get their curious glances in my direction over and done with so that I could put a napkin to my cheek and my hand (*and, oh, God, it's past my wrist? Should I have rolled my sleeves back down, You think?*) in peace.

I twisted to the left in my chair, turning my back to the others in the shop as much as I could without removing my hand from my face or my elbow from the table, awkward as the position was. Guessing, hoping, that no one behind me was paying me any more mind, I snatched up a napkin with my free hand, sliding the napkin up to my wrist and stuffing it between my cheek and its perch in my palm. My gaze then flitted out the window in time to see a rather hot-looking guy walking his mean-looking hulk of a dog past the coffee shop, the guy giving me a quizzical look as he strolled on by.

I finished drying myself off with an inward huff. *Who says it was drool, Mr. Hot Stuff with the Big Mutt? I could've spilled my coffee on myself, for all you know.* Which, I was convinced, would've been a more sophisticated plight.

"Nothing like a good dose of old-fashioned embarrassment to do the trick," I muttered to myself once I was out of the coffee shop and in my car, now wide awake.

All right, not the most favorable episode, but it wasn't my basic idea's fault. I'd try again later. I zipped my car down the street, determined to think right on to my next plan…

The "She" Stands Alone is available as a standalone (☺) and also in a sweet romance collection, ***Inspiring Love: Three Romantic Reads***.

To find all of Nadine's books and her blog featuring book reviews as well as posts on writing, diversity, films, and more, visit:

www.prismaticprospects.wordpress.com

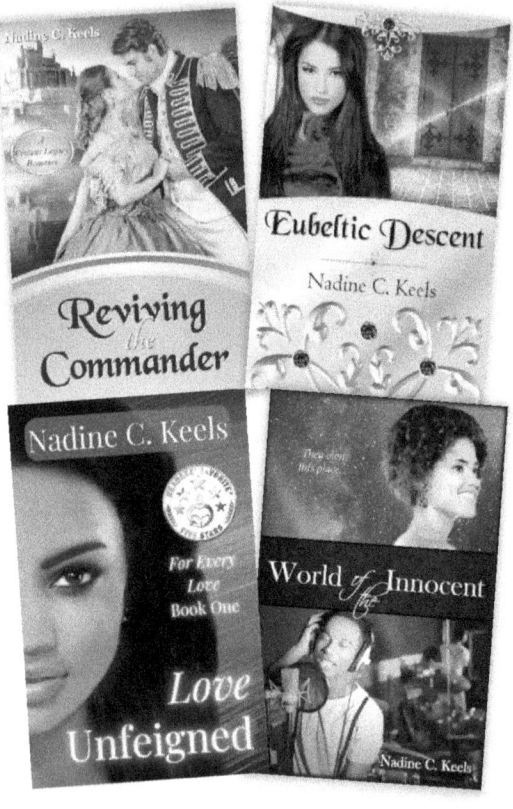

Lightning Source UK Ltd.
Milton Keynes UK
UKHW040612010922
408166UK00004B/330